A NIGHTINGALE SANG

When the Duke held Aleta in his arms, he had never known such rapture.

"Do you love me?" he asked.

"Oh, Tybalt, you know I do."

"You excite me so wildly, my precious."

"I...want to...excite you...as you excite me."

The Duke could only gaze at Aleta's lovely young face.

"Making love is so...wonderful," she whispered.

"My precious, you are sure that is how you felt?"

"Oh, yes and the nightingales were singing... and I am certain the angels were...too."

He held Aleta closer still and said a prayer of thankfulness in his heart.

Looking at her now, her beautiful hair shining in the moonlight, the Duke told himself that no man in the world had ever been more blessed.

"I love you," he cried suddenly. "I love you with all my heart and soul!"

Bantam Books by Barbara Cartland
Ask your bookseller for the books you have missed

Barbara Cartland's Library of Love series

Other Books by Barbara Cartland

A Nightingale Sang

Sang

Barbara Cartland

BANTAM BOOKS · TORONTO · NEW YORK · LONDON

A NIGHTINGALE SANG
A Bantam Book / September 1979

ISBN 0-553-13036-6

Published simultaneously in the United States and Canada

Bantam Books are published by Bantam Books, Inc. Its trademark, consisting of the words "Bantam Books" and the por-
trayal of a bantam, is Registered in U.S. Patent and Trademark
Office and in other countries. Marca Registrada. Bantam
Books, Inc., 666 Fifth Avenue, New York, New York 10019.

PRINTED IN THE UNITED STATES OF AMERICA

Author's Note

When I sang an Album of Love Songs with the Royal Philharmonic Orchestra, I included the most romantic song I know, "A Nightingale Sang in Berkeley Square." Interspersed in each of the love songs are my personal remembrances and poems. This is what I wrote for this one:

This song is full of very special memories for me. I did fall in love in Berkeley Square, and I swear a nightingale sang in the trees as I was kissed.

I remember the scent of lilacs and syringa, the ancient houses silhouetted against the sky, the high trees overhead, the path leading towards a little Temple in the centre of the garden. He was so handsome, and we were both so in love ... with love. There was the magic of the night and of youth, which can never come again, except in our memories.

Chapter One
1919

In the uncurtained windows of the large house in Berkeley Square dancers were silhouetted against a golden background.

The music of the drums and the saxophones throbbed out into the Square as a man came down the steps of the house, and, passing the footmen, the coachmen, and the chauffeurs, who were chatting with one another, crossed the road and entered the Square garden.

Normally the gate in the railings was locked and only the residents of what was one of the most exclusive Squares in London had a key.

Now there were a few couples moving between the bushes of lilac and syringa while the stars shone through the high trees overhead.

The man moved slowly along a small path, obviously deep in thought and taking no notice of anyone he passed.

Finally in the centre of the Square he came to a small Temple surmounted with a Georgian urn, its entrance framed by pillars.

There was only darkness inside and he turned to stand leaning against a pillar and looking back at the ancient trees silhouetted against the sky.

1

He felt in the pocket of his tail-coat for his cigar-case, and as he did so, he heard a very slight movement behind him.

He turned his head, thinking perhaps he was mistaken, then sensed rather than heard that there was somebody there.

With a faint smile on his lips, he asked:

"Am I intruding? In which case I'll go away."

There was a small pause before a hesitant little voice replied:

"N-no ... of course not. I'm ... alone."

The man turned so that now he was facing the inside of the Temple. He realised there was a stone seat and on it sat somebody who was dressed in white.

It was impossible to see her face, but he guessed by the tone of her voice that she was very young.

"Alone?" he asked. "What has happened to your partner?"

"I ... I did not have one. That's why I ... came here."

"No partner?" he questioned. "That is indeed a tragedy, but you are not likely to find one hiding here in the dark."

"I ... know ... but it was so embarrassing ... standing there looking ... expectant, and there seemed to be no extra men."

That, the man knew, was more than likely.

Any unattached men at a party such as he had just left would either be talking to each other, propping up the bar, or would have found their way to the Card-Room.

He thought himself that it was rather a boring Ball in that he knew few people there and there was a mixture of the very grand and the very young, neither of which was to his particular taste.

"I suppose," he said aloud, "as it is the beginning of the Season, that this is your first dance?"

"Yes ... and I was so looking ... forward to it."

"Only to be disappointed. That happens so often

in life when the reality never quite reaches our expectations."

"Surely that's not ... always true?"

"Very often, I find, and then one becomes cynical and disillusioned."

He was joking, but the girl listening to him obviously took him seriously.

"But you mustn't think like that, now that there is no longer a war to make us feel ... frightened and ... apprehensive all the ... time."

"Is that what you felt?"

"Yes."

He was rather glad that she did not elaborate, and he remarked:

"War has its compensations."

"How can you say that?"

"I think I'm entitled to my opinion, having taken part in it."

"You were in Flanders?"

"For four years."

"Oh ... I"

There was silence, then she said:

"It must have been horrible ... terrible! I can't bear to think what our soldiers ... suffered in the ... trenches."

"It was, I admit, extremely unpleasant," the man agreed. "At the same time, there were compensations."

"What were ... they?"

"The comradeship, the sense of having a common purpose in life. It was not only to beat the Germans, but to keep alive, and sometimes one could see the funny side of it all."

"I think you must be very brave."

The man smiled.

"I would like to agree with that statement, but it's not true. I was often very afraid and extremely discontented with my lot."

"Then surely you must be glad ... very glad, that it is all over ... over?"

"Yes, of course, and I'm grateful to have survived such an experience. So many of my friends were killed. To come home is like starting a new life all over again."

"That could be . . . exciting!"

"I wonder. Perhaps I shall find, rather as you are finding your first dance, that it's disappointing."

"It's not really . . . disappointing, in that everything is very . . . beautiful. I have never seen such a magnificent house. The ladies in their jewellery looked so . . . lovely as they danced, but I felt conspicuous because . . . nobody asked me."

"Surely you came with somebody?"

"With my Godmother, with whom I'm staying in London. She's very attractive and all the . . . men who talked to . . . us wanted to dance with . . . her."

The man smiled again a little cynically.

He could understand so well what had happened. He had been told that the days of Chaperones were over, and any mothers, aunts, or, as in this case, a Godmother, who accompanied débutantes were invited as dancers.

He could imagine the girl being left a forelorn little wall-flower of no particular interest to anyone.

He walked farther into the Temple and, guided more by instinct than sight, sat down on the stone seat beside the girl.

He knew she gave a little quiver as he did so, and he thought she must be very young and very inexperienced, and he found it rather pathetic.

"You're not alone now," he said, "and as I, like you, knew very few people here, we can console each other."

"Perhaps it is . . . wrong."

"Wrong?" he questioned.

"We have not been . . . introduced."

He laughed.

"That makes it all the easier. We'll just pretend that you are the goddess of the Temple, and I'm an explorer who has discovered you."

"You make it . . . sound very . . . exciting."

"Perhaps it will be. Tell me what you feel now that you are grown up and have presumably left School."

"I didn't go to School. I was educated by a Governess."

"Was she a good one?"

"She was not particularly clever, but I like reading and I thought I knew a little bit about the world . . . only to find I'm very ignorant about . . . dances and how one should . . . behave."

"What you need is a nice young man to look after you. I understand the war has swept away all the old conventions, and girls can go out dancing alone with a young man."

"Only if they are . . . invited to do so."

He laughed again.

"I stand corrected. Of course, only if they are invited to do so. And as you've only just come to London, you do not know anyone to ask you."

"That is right."

"Shall I promise you that every day, every week, things will get better? I am quite certain you'll soon find a lot of young men eager to invite you to dance with them."

"How can you say that . . . when you have not . . . seen me?"

"I'm a judge of voices, and as I think your voice is very attractive, I'm quite certain its owner is attractive too."

It was a rather banal comment, the man thought as he said it, but he knew she stiffened nervously, rather like a foal, he thought, who is not certain if it can trust the hand put out to pat it.

"I hope you are . . . right," she said after a moment, "but you see, now that I've come to London it seems so . . . big and in some ways . . . frightening. I know I will make a great many . . . mistakes."

"We all make mistakes when we do anything new," the man said. "I remember when I joined my

Regiment I was terrified that I would do something contrary to tradition which would make me the laughing-stock of the other Subalterns."

"And . . . did you?"

"Nothing terribly ludicrous, but I know exactly what you're feeling, and in time that will pass."

"You are very comforting."

"I want to be. You see, you're starting a new life with everything fresh about it. I have to pick up the threads of an old one and in a way that is more difficult."

"How can it be?"

"I suppose it is because there is so much I have missed, for which I have a certain amount of regret."

The girl gave a little sigh.

"Just at this . . . moment I wish I were . . . five years . . . older."

The man laughed and it was a genuine sound of amusement.

"In five years you'll not be saying that! You'll begin to worry in case you're getting old, and in ten years' time you'll be taking five years off your age."

"Is that what women do? Yes, I believe you are right! I'm sure my Godmother is older than she says she is."

"Well, that's one thing you need not worry about —not yet."

"I hope by the time I get older I shall not have to . . . worry about such . . . trivial things."

"Women do not think them trivial. To them they are very important."

"And to men?"

"Men have much more serious worries, especially at this moment."

"I suppose, by saying that, you're looking for a job?"

"That is perceptive of you. How did you know?"

"Everybody is saying how difficult it is for men coming out of the Services to find anything to do. Men who managed to wangle themselves into reserved occupations and stayed at home have taken over all the best jobs, and now that the soldiers are demobbed, they are looking for employment which, my father says, does not exist."

"Your father is quite right. That is what I've discovered."

"I am so ... sorry for you. What do you ... want to do?"

"To tell the truth, I really have no idea, but I have to make some money."

"I think that is going to be ... difficult."

"That is what I have already found."

There was a pause, then he said:

"Now let us talk about you. I can predict your future quite easily."

"How?"

"Well, you'll find your feet, you'll find a charming young man, and you'll get married."

She sighed.

"I know that is what everybody will ... expect me to do ... but I am ... afraid."

"Afraid?"

"I do not want to marry ... anybody, unless I am ... really in love."

"And how do you think you will know if you are in love?"

"I have thought about it ... and I know it will be something very wonderful and very ... different from what I have ever felt before. It'll not be just ... wanting to dance with someone or even to be with them. It'll be more than that."

"In what way?"

"It is difficult to put into words, but I think it'll be something beautiful ... like the mist over the lake ... or the first evening star when the sky still has the glow of the sun in it."

There was a little quiver in the girl's voice. Then she said:

"When I was walking ... here alone tonight to ... hide in this Temple, I could see the stars overhead ... and I thought, although I might have been mistaken, that I heard nightingales ... singing in the trees."

"And you think that will be part of your love?"

"I think what I shall feel will be something like that, only more ... rapturous ... more perfect ... but then ... real love must come from ... God."

"You believe in God?"

"Yes, of course. Don't you?"

"Shall I say I want to believe in Him? But I found it hard in the mud and stench of the trenches to believe He cared a damn what was happening to us all."

"But He did! I am sure He did. After all ... we won the war!"

"At a terrible cost."

He felt her make a little movement and he knew that she had clenched her fingers together. Then she said:

"But you ... are alive."

"Yes, I am alive."

"And so somehow you and ... others who have ... survived have to make ... something of the peace."

"I think the Politicians have already made a mess of it."

"You must not let them. You must make certain, after so much suffering, that those who ... died did not do so in ... vain."

"Who has talked to you about such things?"

"No-one ... but I read the newspapers."

"That's unusual. I thought young women only thought of clothes, and of course—love."

"I have had very few clothes to think about, and I only know of ... love from what I have ... read."

There was a pause, then she asked:

"Are you ... laughing at what I said ... just now?"

"No, no! Of course not! You are absolutely right. That is the love you should seek, and what I would want you to look for. I only hope that the man, when you find him and fall in love, will not fail you."

"Perhaps . . . I shall . . . fail him."

"I think that is unlikely."

"Why?"

"Because most young women, at least the ones I have met, are not so idealistic as you are."

"I am . . . grateful to you for not saying . . . 'romantic.'"

"Why?"

"I think 'romance' is a horrid word, sentimental and rather sloppy, and I am sure the love I . . . want is very . . . different."

"It will be."

"How can you be . . . sure?"

"I'm very sure. And I predict that you will find your ideal man and be very happy with him."

"Suppose I don't find him?"

"Then I suppose, like most people, you'll have to settle for second best."

"I should hate that! I think it would be a betrayal of . . . everything in which I believe!"

There was almost a passionate intensity in the young voice, and the man said:

"If you set your sights too high, if you try to touch the stars, then you are bound to be disappointed, and I should hate that to happen to you."

"Are you really advising me to accept . . . second best? I would somehow not expect . . . you to say that."

"Why not?"

"When we were talking of the war I thought you sounded rather like one of the Knights of the days of Chivalry who fought because they were fighting for Christianity, or perhaps seeking the . . . Holy Grail."

"Many years ago perhaps I felt like that, but now I have forgotten the dreams I dreamt and the Crusades I wanted to join."

"They'll come back to you. We never really forget them, because they are ... part of ... ourselves."

The man thought for a moment, then he said:

"When I came here and first talked to you, I thought you were very, very young; but now I am beginning to think you are old and wise in many things that other people have either not known or have forgotten."

"Now you *are* laughing at ... me!"

"No, I promise you I am not. I think perhaps you are not real and I'm sitting here alone talking to my conscience, or my heart, whichever you would like to be."

"I would like to be both. It is a lovely idea."

"You have certainly made me think."

"You have made me think too, and I am not as frightened as I was of this ... new world."

"That's right. Do not be frightened of it. Just tell yourself you will conquer it. At the same time, you must not let it spoil you."

"Why should it spoil me?"

"Because it may make you think that what you value at the moment is worthless, and that the glittering tinsel you will find all round you is more important, more real. But it's not!"

"How will I be able to tell the ... real from the ... false?"

"Your instinct will tell you that, so follow your instinct. That's the best advice I can give you, for I am convinced that you know your way better than I know mine."

"You know that's not true."

"In a strange way it is."

There was silence. Then the girl said:

"I suppose I ... ought to go ... back. My Godmother may ... wonder what has ... happened to me."

"She should look after you better and she should certainly introduce you to some partners."

"She tried, but as soon as she had done so, they ... slipped away. I think perhaps I do not ... look quite right."

"That is something which is easily remedied. What is right is your thinking, so hold on to that."

"I will . . . try."

She made a little movement and began to rise to her feet.

The man put out his hand and touched her arm.

"No, do not go," he said. "I want to go first because I think it would spoil things for both of us if we saw each other. We have talked and you have opened up new horizons for me."

"And you for . . . me."

"Very well, let us leave it at that. If I take you back and dance with you, we may both be disillusioned, and that, I think, would be a mistake."

"Yes, of course."

"I want to go first, but incidentally, I'm not going back to the dance. I'm going to walk, think of what we've said to each other, and look at my future in a different way from what I've done before."

"I hope you'll find . . . everything you . . . seek."

"Perhaps you have given me an idea of what I am seeking. I don't know yet. I have to think about it by myself."

"I shall . . . think too."

"Yes, do that, but remember, above everything I've told you, not to let anything spoil you. Hold on to your ideals, and never, never accept second best."

The man rose as he spoke and she looked up, seeing his dark outline, realising that he was tall and broad-shouldered. Then he put out his hand and drew her to her feet.

"I want to wish you luck," he said, "and I want, too, to say good-bye to my heart and my conscience."

He pulled her closer to him as he spoke.

She did not struggle or try to prevent him, and he had an idea that she was feeling as he was: that it was all unreal.

Then very gently, as a man might kiss a flower, he found her lips.

It was a kiss that might have been part of a dream, almost inhuman, and yet the softness and

innocence of her mouth was an enchantment he had
never known before in his whole life.

Instinctively his arms tightened, his lips became
a little more possessive, and he felt a quiver go
through her.

Then resolutely, without speaking, he released
her, turned, and walked from the Temple into the
garden.

He walked towards the gate, not looking back,
but as he went he was almost certain he heard a
nightingale singing overhead in the trees.

*   *   *

1921

Down the long drive Sir Harry Wayte had his
first glimpse of his house ahead, and as he did so he
thought that there was no place in the whole world
quite so attractive or so beautiful.

Kings Wayte had been built early in the reign
of Elizabeth I, but it was not until Charles II stayed
there a century later that he changed its name.

Owing to difficulties on the road and the incom-
petence of his staff, the King's mistress, who was due
to join him at a party given by the owner of the
house, had not arrived until long after she was due.

"My impatience has grown with every hour that
has passed," he told her when she finally arrived.

"Your Majesty had to wait through no fault of
mine!" she retorted.

The King had laughed.

"Whoever we blame, I was still kept waiting," he
said. "In the future this house will always remain in
my memory as the King's Wait."

Sir Harry's ancestor had thought such a christen-
ing an amusing jest, and the family house of the
Waytes had from that time forward been known as
"Kings Wayte."

There had been rich Waytes, poor Waytes,
Waytes who had squandered their money, and those
who had hoarded it.

But as Sir Harry drove across the bridge that spanned the lake, he thought that there had never been a Wayte who was quite as impecunious as he was at this moment.

As if the car which he was driving wished to express its own feelings, it began to backfire, then to move jerkily forward until it came to a standstill a few yards from the front door.

Before Sir Harry could get out, a girl came running down the steps.

"Harry, you are here!" she exclaimed. "I was worried in case something had happened to you."

"I've had the devil of a time, Aleta," her brother answered. "As far as I can make out, the car's only firing on one cylinder, and I have run out of petrol!"

"Hitchen will see to it. You are here, and that is all that matters."

Harry got out of the car, pulling off his cap and goggles as he did so.

It was an open and very ancient vehicle, a 1910 model that he had bought cheap and which had given him endless trouble ever since he had owned it.

But then, as he had said often enough, what could you expect for the small amount of money he could afford to pay?

His sister slipped her arm through his and drew him up the steps.

"Tea's waiting for you, and if you are hungry you can have a boiled egg."

"No . . . I'll wait for dinner. You look distressingly thin. What have you been doing to yourself?"

"There has been an awful lot to do in the house, and I suppose too I have been worrying."

"Can we do anything else?"

"I suppose not."

"I have a solution which will stop us from worrying for a little while, but you may not like it."

His sister looked at him apprehensively.

Harry threw his cap and goggles down on a

chair and pushed his fair hair back from his fore-head.

He was a handsome young man, and there was a faint resemblance between brother and sister, for Aleta was also fair, but her eyes, which seemed to fill her small pointed face, were grey while her brother's were blue.

"Come and tell me all about it," she said. "Then I have some bad news for you."

"Bad news?" Harry asked quickly.

"The ceiling has fallen down in the Tapestry-Room. I heard a crash in the night and wondered what it could be. You have never seen such a mess!"

"That's the third in the last month. We'll have to get them repaired."

"Repaired! How can we afford that?"

"That is what I am just going to tell you."

Aleta looked at him apprehensively as they walked into a large and beautifully proportioned room with diamond-paned casements overlooking the lawns which sloped down to the lake.

It was a room with an atmosphere, and the furniture was part of it and had been there for generations.

But the carpet was nearly threadbare and the curtains had faded to a very pale echo of the rose pink they had once been.

There was a tea-table in the window and on it was a silver tray containing a silver tea-pot with the Wayte crest on it.

It looked somehow surprisingly small, and the milk-jug and sugar-basin were not of the same period.

Aleta, as she sat down at the table, forced herself not to think of the beautiful George III set which they had sold only a month ago.

She poured out a cup of tea for her brother and one for herself, then she said:

"You said you had a ... solution."

He knew, by the tone of her voice and the anxiety in her eyes, what she feared, and he said quickly:

"No, I am not intending to abandon the house—not yet."

"Oh, Harry, I lay awake all last night worrying in case that was what you meant to do. I could not bear to watch Kings Wayte fall down!"

"We may have to do so later," Harry replied. "How could father have died owing so much money?"

It was a question which they had asked themselves thousands of times already, and although Aleta knew there were some more or less reasonable answers, she did not bother to make them. She merely waited for Harry to explain himself.

"What I have to say," he said tentatively, taking a cucumber sandwich from the plate in front of him, "may shock you. At the same time, I think you will agree that it has possibilities."

Aleta drew in her breath but did not speak.

"I have a chance to let the house for a year!"

The words seemed almost to be forced from between Harry's lips, and there was an uncomfortable silence until Aleta said faintly:

"Let . . . it? But to whom?"

"An American."

Then quickly, as if he thought he had better get it over, Harry said:

"It was Cosgrove who suggested it. I was in the Club, wondering if I could afford to buy myself a drink, and he came up to me and said:

" 'Hello, Wayte. I wanted to see you.'

" 'What about?' I asked.

" 'I know you own one of the finest houses in England, and it's just what I am looking for at the moment.'

" 'Looking for?' I echoed rather stupidly.

" 'I have an American client who wants to come over here and do things in style. As a matter of fact, he intends to marry off his daughter to a Duke. It is a pity you are not a Marquess or an Earl, otherwise he might have settled for you!' "

Harry paused, then he said:

"I felt like punching him for his impertinence, but you know Cosgrove. That sort of joke is his sense of humour."

Aleta had never met Cosgrove, but her brother had spoken of him often enough.

He had set himself up as a kind of universal provider and was making a lot of money out of it.

He had been in the same Regiment as Harry, and while other Officers wandered round wondering what they should do when the war was over, Captain Charles Cosgrove had made himself a go-between, a Purchasing Agent, with a success which gave him the reputation of being able to obtain everything anyone might require.

If a friend wanted a reliable hunter, he found it; if someone else wanted a cheap or an expensive car, Cosgrove procured it.

There were even rumours that he had the telephone numbers of some very attractive women, but this piece of information Harry had not passed on to his sister.

Now he continued:

"I was just about to say I wouldn't think of letting Kings Wayte, especially to an American, when Cosgrove said:

" 'My client is prepared to pay through the nose, and I mean that! I thought of asking him for five thousand pounds for the rent and everything extra on top of that.' "

"Five thousand pounds!" Aleta exclaimed. "He could not have said that!"

"He did, and it took my breath away," Harry admitted. "Then he explained that Wardolf—that is the American's name—is a millionaire several times over. He owns half the railroads in America and so many oil-wells that even Cosgrove has lost count of them!"

"But . . . five thousand . . . pounds!" Aleta said barely above a whisper.

"I thought you would be impressed," Harry said, "but there's more to it than that."

"In what way?"

"Apparently this American has no wife, and he wants the house to be in perfect running-order for himself and his daughter. He intends to entertain in a big way and he wants us to provide the servants, the horses, the cars, the gardeners, and every other facility you can think of."

Aleta was speechless, and she could only stare at her brother as he went on:

"It is not going to be easy, and we have only a month in which to prepare everything before he arrives at the end of May."

"But, Harry . . . !"

"I know, I know!" her brother interrupted. "But Cosgrove says we can spend anything we like in getting the house ready. We can paint, repair, buy new linen and new carpets if we want to. All Wardolf wants is to be able to stay here and give huge parties to introduce his daughter to the right people."

Harry grinned.

"Cosgrove will see to that! Of that you can be sure."

"But . . . how can we? It is . . . impossible!"

"We have to make it posssible, because as you and I well know, we can not only do with five thousand pounds, but all the other pickings as well. Think what it would mean to have a new carpet in this room, for instance."

"But, Harry, how can we find workmen, servants, and all the other things in a month?"

"We have to, and what is more, I was thinking as I came down that we shall have to supervise everything ourselves."

"You mean . . . stay on here with our . . . tenants?"

Harry was silent. Then he said:

"You are not going to like this, Aleta, but it was

Cosgrove's idea that you and I should stay to run things. Incognito, so to speak."

"I . . . do not . . . understand."

"Then let me put it very plainly. You will be the person who runs the house, and I will see to everything else."

"You said . . . incognito."

"That is exactly what I meant. Obviously it would be embarrassing for the Americans if they knew we owned the place, so we have to pretend that we are the servants of the owner and are acting on his behalf. The only problem is deciding what we shall call ourselves."

Aleta rose to her feet.

"I think you're mad! We cannot do it! We shall be found out! The whole thing is an impossibility!"

Harry's lips tightened. Then he said slowly:

"Not if we have unlimited money to spend."

"Unlimited?"

"That is what Cosgrove said. As a matter of fact, he is in a fix. He has tried all the other big houses near London, which is where Wardolf wishes to be, and there is not one available. This is his last hope, and he is determined not to lose the very large commission he will get on all the arrangements. And he will help us in every possible manner, you can be sure of that."

"And I would be . . . the . . . Housekeeper!"

"You know as well as I do that we could not have a lot of strange servants mixed up with our old lot unless there is someone to give the orders, to keep everything running smoothly."

This was irrefutable, and Aleta was silent, knowing that the few elderly women left in the house, whom they could not afford to pension off, would never get on with strangers, or know what to do, unless she was there.

It was not, she felt, that the position would be ignominious. It was just that the whole thing seemed such a colossal task that she was afraid of the vast amount of detail that must be seen to.

She knew better than Harry the state the house was in. It had been left to crumble during the war, with only a few very ancient retainers to look after herself and her Governess.

Most of the time their father had lived in London, having a vague job at the War Office which was never very clearly defined.

He had died last year and they had both been appalled to find the amount of money he owed.

When Harry had returned from France, where he had been the last year of the war, he had nearly cried when he saw not only the state of the house but also the stables and the gardens.

"When I think what it used to be like," he kept saying to Aleta, and she too had felt like crying.

In order to live and to pay off their father's creditors, to whom they had promised some sort of repayment month by month, it had been necessary to sell many of their precious possessions.

It had broken Harry's heart, Aleta knew, not only to part with the silver that had been in the family for generations but also a number of the paintings.

She knew, although neither of them mentioned it, that because a particularly fine Gainsborough had gone to America they could neither of them think of that country without feeling something suspiciously like hatred.

Yet it was an American who would now move into Kings Wayte, and Aleta found herself already resenting it, although she knew she was being foolish.

"Have you really ... decided to do this?" she asked.

"What alternative is there," he replied, "except to sell more paintings?"

She knew that he was fighting to keep other family portraits, done by Reynolds and Lawrence, which they both loved but which they knew day after day grew nearer to going under the Auctioneer's hammer.

It was the thought of the Gainsborough that made Aleta make up her mind.

"I'll do anything for five thousand pounds!"

"And let us not forget all the repairs and the redecoration also," Harry added.

"You will have to repair the stables. You couldn't put a horse or even a car under the holes in the roof."

"I realise that."

He put his hand in his inner pocket and drew out a piece of paper, which he lay down on the tea-table.

Aleta looked down. It was a cheque for a thousand pounds.

"Oh, Harry . . .!"

"That is for our immediate expenses," he explained. "Cosgrove said any big bills, like repairs, furnishings, and anything else we need to buy, we can send to him."

Aleta's grey eyes widened.

She was just beginning to understand what this would mean, and she felt a little wave of excitement sweep over her.

"I cannot . . . believe it's true! You must be . . . making it all up."

"It is true," Harry replied, "and though it may be damned awkward in some ways, turning ourselves into superior servants and being ordered about by an American, we shall just have to remember that it will pay off most of Father's debts and Kings Wayte will get the repairs it badly needs."

Aleta sat down beside him again and put her arms round his neck.

"If we can do that, it would be worth working as a galley-slave. Oh, Harry, I have worried terribly, thinking that the only solution would be to sell the house and the Estate."

"As a matter of fact I cannot do that," Harry said. "I know we have talked about it, but it is entailed—not that I shall ever be able to afford to have a son!"

There were tears in Aleta's eyes, but her lips were smiling.

"Our luck has changed!" she said. "It is just as if a huge black cloud has lifted and we are sitting in the sunshine! Now nothing will have to go, not even the other Gainsborough."

Harry smiled too.

"I cannot do this without your help."

"Of course I will help you. And it will be fun because we will be doing it together. We shall have to start work right away."

"That is what I thought," Harry agreed, "so I stopped in the village on the way here. Johnson says he will be up to see us within the hour."

"Then he had better bring his tools with him," Aleta said with a laugh. "He is going to need them!"

men from all over the County and they had been

Chapter Two

Aleta gave a deep sigh and sat down on the
sofa.

"I can't do any more!" she said. "And if anything's not to their satisfaction, they are just going to
have to put up with it!"

"You've been marvellous!" Harry said. "I've told
Johnson that all his men shall have a bonus. They
have really done miracles!"

"They have indeed," Aleta agreed, "and the house
looks quite different."

She glanced round the Drawing-Room as she
spoke, thinking that with its new curtains and carpet
it had a new beauty, and she wished her father could
have seen it.

The carpet was in fact only hired, because it was
a valuable Persian which they could not have afforded, but Captain Cosgrove had, in his usual
miraculous manner, filled their need.

Aleta had arranged masses of flowers which
brightened even the dullest rooms which they had
not had time to redecorate.

The same applied upstairs. A large number of
the bedrooms looked very presentable but there was
still a lot more to be done, which was not surprising
considering that Kings Wayte had over three hundred
rooms.

Nevertheless, as Harry had said, Johnson, the
local carpenter and decorator, had collected work-

men from all over the County and they had been wise to put their trust in him.

He had known Kings Wayte all his life, had loved it, and had done any repairs they could afford ever since their father had inherited it from his father.

Not only would he have been bitterly hurt if they had gone elsewhere, as Captain Cosgrove had suggested, but from no-one else would they have received the same attention and interest.

That also applied to their other arrangements.

Aleta had been determined that the old servants who had been loyal to them all through the war should not be upset by the importation of London types who would doubtless have looked down their noses at them and made trouble.

She had therefore insisted, even though Harry was dubious that it would be successful, not only on persuading many of their old pensioners to come back and help but on enlisting young girls from the village and other parts of the Estate.

"The older ones will teach them," she said, "and I shall be there to see what must be done."

"I've been thinking about that," Harry said, "and I'm convinced that you ought to keep out of sight as much as possible."

Aleta laughed.

"That has been my idea too, but perhaps not for the same reasons."

"I consider it important because you look so young and are far too pretty. I can't have our American guests making eyes at you."

Aleta thought the same thing and she had no desire to put herself into an embarrassing situation. What she had done, therefore, was to persuade their former Housekeeper, who had been at Kings Wayte for over forty years, to come back out of retirement.

Harry had at first been horrified at the idea.

"Old Mrs. Abbott?" he exclaimed. "I thought she was dead!"

"No, she isn't," Aleta replied. "She is living with

her sister in St. Albans. I'll go and see her and tell her I want her to help."

"But she must be a hundred!" Harry exclaimed. "At least that's what I always thought when I was a child."

"She is getting on for eighty," Aleta admitted, "but as long as she can move on her two feet, I am determined she shall be here. The Americans can then give their orders to her and she can pass them on to me."

Harry finally gave in simply because he did not wish to be bothered, having enough to occupy his mind in getting the stables repaired and engaging grooms and chauffeurs.

He had been astounded, as Aleta had, at the amount of staff which Charles Cosgrove said the Americans would require.

"Four chauffeurs," Harry had exclaimed, "besides the one who will bring them down? What can they want with so many?"

"The very rich expect to spend money," Charles Cosgrove had answered. "In America, Wardolf has a private train, a fleet of cars, motor-boats, yachts, and even an aeroplane ready to carry him wherever he wishes to go at a moment's notice."

"No-one should be as rich as that!" Harry muttered, but Charles Cosgrove had laughed.

"You wouldn't refuse to be in the same position yourself, but you have something which Mr. Cornelius Wardolf will never have."

"What is that?" Aleta asked curiously.

"A home that is not only a perfect architectural monument but belongs to you and yours, plus the fact that your family tree will turn him green with envy."

They all laughed, but when Aleta thought about it later she knew that Captain Cosgrove was right.

No money could buy the history which lay behind her and Harry. No money could build a house like Kings Wayte, with its atmosphere, its ghosts, and its mellow beauty which had come with centuries of time.

"I love it!" Aleta told herself, looking at the sunshine on the lake.

She knew that as far as she was concerned no other place could be so perfect and nowhere else would she feel as if she belonged.

'Whatever sacrifices Harry and I have to make, they are worthwhile,' she thought.

She knew she ought to be grateful, humbly grateful, for the fact that thanks to Mr. Cornelius Wardolf they would not have to worry so much about their future, at least for a year.

After her father had died she had felt, when they learnt what the situation was, that she and Harry were fighting a hopeless battle in which inevitably they would finally be defeated.

And yet now, like a blessing out of the blue, there had come a reprieve, and she felt as if every nail that the workmen put into the ancient building, every tile they put on the roof, every pane of glass that was set back into the casement windows, brought her another little glimmer of hope.

Perhaps somehow, in some unforeseeable way, they would be able to go on living at Kings Wayte and not have to watch it crumbling to the ground as she had thought they must do a month ago.

"Thank You, thank You, God," she said every morning as she rose very early to start work.

She said the same words as she curled up in bed at night to fall asleep almost before she had finished her prayers.

"What time are they arriving?" she asked Harry now, and glanced at the clock on the mantelpiece, which was running for the first time since the beginning of the war.

"In about an hour's time. Is there anything else you want taken up to the Nurseries? If so, I'll do it for you."

"I think I've remembered everything," Aleta replied.

When they had realised that they would have to move out of their own rooms, they had held a conference to decide where they should go.

It was Aleta who felt she could not bear to move into the servants' quarters and had the bright idea of opening the Nurseries on the third floor.

"It'll be rather fun to sleep where we did as children; at least the rooms are familiar and we won't feel like aliens in our own home."

Harry had agreed but had not been particularly interested.

But Aleta knew there would doubtless be long hours when she would be alone, and it was somehow comforting to think she could sit in front of the Nursery fire, with its brass-edged guard, in the chair that Nanny had always occupied, with the screen covered in transfers and Christmas cards to keep out the draughts behind her.

She had taken up all the possessions she could not bear anyone else to touch: things which had belonged to her mother and the books that had been her father's favourites.

One thing she regretted leaving more than anything else was the huge Library.

Even during the war she had insisted that the servants keep that room open and dust it occasionally so that she could look over the books on the shelves.

When she had picked one, she would curl up on the window-seat to read it.

'I can still help myself to what I want,' she thought, 'because no-one will notice. At the same time, it will not be the same as sitting in the place I have always sat, knowing that if the book doesn't please, there are thousands more to choose from.'

These were minor regrets.

What was so exciting was to see how different the old house looked with new curtains in the main rooms and hired carpets on the floors or rugs to cover the more threadbare patches.

Charles Cosgrove had had the brilliant idea of going to the Sale-Rooms to buy curtains which, if a little worn, were not in the dilapidated state of those at Kings Wayte.

"So many people have given up their big houses in the war, or can't afford to live in them now," he said, "that you can obtain curtains and furniture at knock-down prices."

"Who can afford to buy them?" Aleta asked.

Captain Cosgrove smiled a little cynically.

"Need you ask?" he said. "The Americans are bargain-hunting in Europe. I'm told the Duke of Westminster, who is richer than any of the other Dukes, is selling his *Blue Boy*."

"Oh no! How can he?" Aleta asked angrily. "That painting belongs to England. They've no right to let it go across the Atlantic."

Captain Cosgrove shrugged his shoulders.

"I suppose he needs the money, like everyone else, and if you'd not insisted on having local footmen, I could have produced any number of ex-Officers who don't deem it beneath them to wait on the *nouveaux riches*."

"Is it still so difficult to get jobs?" Aleta asked in her soft voice.

"Almost impossible!" Captain Cosgrove replied. "And those who have sunk their annuity into chicken-farms and such-like are all going bankrupt. If I wanted to employ a thousand men, I could get them by raising my finger."

His words made Aleta wonder whether the man she had talked to over a year ago in the Temple in Berkeley Square had found the employment he was seeking.

She had found it impossible to forget that strange enchanted night when she had been kissed for the first and only time in her life and when she had heard the nightingales singing in the trees overhead.

Looking back, it seemed to her like a beautiful dream from which she had not awakened too soon but which had faded slowly into wakefulness, never to be forgotten.

She went over and over again every word of the

conversation she had had with the man who had sat
beside her but whom she had never seen.

She wondered what he looked like, and thought
that because his voice was deep and compelling and
he was tall and had square shoulders, he would be
dark and handsome.

She was glad she had not seen him, because
then he would have seen her, and although he had
said that because her voice was attractive she must
be attractive too, he might have been disappointed.

Sometimes she looked at herself in the mirror
and wondered how much she had changed since that
night when, lost, shy, and very unsure of herself,
she had slipped away from her first Ball and found
in the little Temple in the garden a magic that was
unforgettable.

How could she have known, how could she have
guessed, that such an adventure was waiting for her?

But because of what a stranger had said to her,
everything had seemed changed and she had gone
back to the Ball with a smile on her lips and had
danced quite a number of times before her Godmother was ready to go home.

After that the social round had not been so
difficult.

She felt sometimes as if she had been in a little
boat which the man in the Temple had pushed
out into the stream, and she had found, because he
had done so, that she could sail quite competently.

She had not had a great deal of time to find out
what London held for her, for a month after that
dance in Berkeley Square she had received a tele-
gram from home to say that her father was ill.

She had hurried to Kings Wayte and one look
at her father told her he was very ill indeed.

She had sent for Harry, who was in the process
of leaving his Regiment, and he too had rushed to
his father's bedside.

Sir Hugo had caught the virulent influenza
which had swept over Europe and had actually
taken more lives than had been lost in the war.

In Sir Hugo's case, influenza had turned to pneumonia, and it was from that disease that he had finally died.

It was then that Harry and Aleta learnt their true financial circumstances. From then on there was no question of Balls or parties, but of a desperate effort to live and to keep those who were dependent upon them from starving.

There were pensioners to be paid and servants to be fed, and as Harry had said despairingly: "Damned little with which to do it!"

Of course things had to be sold, and each painting taken off the wall, each piece of silver taken from the Pantry safe, was, Aleta thought, like cutting off a part of their own bodies.

She knew the history of everything they had to dispose of, and all of them seemed to have special links with her personally, and she knew Harry felt the same.

When the paintings were collected by the Dealer who bought them, Harry went out riding early in the morning and didn't come back until it was dark.

It was Aleta who had to watch them driven off in a van that clattered over the stone bridge, which needed repointing, and up the drive where potholes made the vehicle rock from side to side as the wheels went in and out of them.

"What else must go? What else?" she had asked herself.

She thought now that for a year it would not be a question which need be echoing in her mind.

"You look all in," Harry said solicitously. "I'm going to get you a drink. What would you like?"

"If you give me anything alcoholic I shall feel dizzy," Aleta replied. "You know, neither of us has had time to eat anything today."

"I didn't even think about it!" Harry said in surprise. "I was so busy."

He got to his feet, then gave a sudden shout.

"I've an idea!"

"What is it?"

"You and I are going to accept the hospitality of our tenant by opening a bottle of his very excellent champagne!"

"Oh, Harry, you can't do that."

"I have every intention of doing it," Harry replied, "and if you feel it is dishonest, let me tell you that as I helped carry the crates downstairs I am at least entitled to the wages of an ordinary labourer, and that would be a great deal higher than one bottle of champagne!"

He left the room before Aleta could reply, and as she leant back against a newly covered satin cushion she thought that she had never been so tired in her whole life.

In the past, after a hard day's riding beside her father she had been weary, but now every muscle in her body ached and her brain felt as if it no longer belonged to her.

She knew it was because she had been driving herself, as Harry had, practically twenty-four hours a day, but it was worth every moment of it to see Kings Wayte being restored to the beauty that they had known in her grandfather's time.

Unfortunately, it had not been his money which had enabled him to live in great style in the family house, but his wife's, and he only had the spending of her income.

When she died, her capital was retained by her own family.

'Since then it's always been save, save, save,' Aleta thought, 'and trying to make ends meet.'

Then she told herself a little wryly that her father had not tried very hard. He had just gone on spending on what had seemed to him to be necessities, leaving them to clear up the mess after he was dead.

'At least he enjoyed himself,' Aleta thought, 'as Harry will enjoy himself now, for a year.'

She knew that what had pleased her brother more than anything else were the horses he had been told to buy.

"Does Mr. Wardolf ride?" he had enquired of Charles Cosgrove.

"I have no idea," was the reply, "but I gather he expects every English facility to be open to him, and that, as you well know, includes horses."

Harry needed no persuading to fill the stables, and Aleta knew that whatever else happened, he would take the opportunity of exercising the horses, which delighted him by their breeding and by their performance over the jumps he had set up in the park.

"I've spent a fortune today," he said when he returned from the sales at Tattersall's, "and Cosgrove paid up for everything I purchased without turning a hair!"

"I only hope Mr. Wardolf will do the same," Aleta said, a little touch of fear in her voice. "Just suppose, Harry, that he says he doesn't like what we've bought for him and refuses to pay?"

"That's Cosgrove's fault, not ours," Harry said. "Stop worrying. If you ask me, if there are any complaints it'll be because we've been too sparing, not too extravagant."

It was Captain Cosgrove who pointed out one shortcoming at Kings Wayte.

"There is one thing the Americans are certain to miss," he said, when he was complimenting them on everything they had done.

"What's that?" Harry asked.

"A swimming-bath."

For a moment both Harry and Aleta looked blank, then Harry said:

"Do they really find one necessary?"

"Americans love bathing," Captain Cosgrove replied, "but I'm afraid they won't think much of the only two bathrooms you have here. I don't mind betting you he'll order some more as soon as he arrives."

"I hope not," Harry said. "We had enough trouble getting the pipes to work as it is."

"Americans are a very clean people," Captain Cosgrove said with a grin.

"But who uses the swimming-bath?"

"Everyone!" he replied. "Including those who go to the rowdy Hollywood parties and usually end up in them fully dressed."

"It sounds a very unpleasant way to amuse one-self," Aleta said coldly.

"I hope they're not going to have those sort of parties here," Harry said. "If they damage anything they'll have to pay for it."

"That's agreed already," Captain Cosgrove said. "I put a clause in the lease to make sure of that. In fact, with any luck, when they leave you'll get quite a lot of carpets and coverings replaced whether they damage them or not."

Harry saw Aleta look up as if she was going to protest, and he said quickly:

"That's all right. I know we can trust you, Charles, to look after our interests."

"I hope I've done that," Captain Cosgrove replied, "and my own as well."

When he had gone, Aleta said to her brother:

"I know he has been very kind, but I don't really like Captain Cosgrove. There's something about him which makes me feel he thinks of everything in terms of pounds, shillings, and pence."

"And very wisely," Harry retorted. "If he hadn't done so, he'd have gone under, as so many chaps in my Regiment have done. Henson shot himself last week."

"Oh . . . no!" Aleta said in horror.

"He couldn't get a job, so his wife left him. He was always a rather hysterical sort of fellow."

"It is so wrong . . . so cruel!" Aleta said passionately, "that men who fought for this country are now penniless and unable to fend for themselves. The Government should do something about it."

It was a cry which the newspapers echoed every day, but nothing seemed to be done, and although it was difficult to find out the facts, Aleta gathered that there was vast unemployment over the whole country.

'Perhaps after all we should be grateful to the Americans,' she thought.

At the same time, it seemed unfair, for although they too had suffered heavy casualties, they had come out of the war richer than when they went into it.

She finished off her glass of champagne and said:

"Thank you for that, Harry. Now I think I should go upstairs. I don't want Mr. Wardolf to arrive and find me sitting here."

"Certainly not!" Harry agreed. "I'll join you in a few minutes."

Aleta walked from the Drawing-Room into the Hall and saw four footmen, wearing the Wayte livery with its large crested silver buttons, standing rather self-consciously by the front door.

They grinned at her in a slightly familiar manner because they were all lads from the village. They had been drilled every day by old Barlow, who had been the Butler at Kings Wayte before the war, and although he was nearly seventy-five he was delighted to be back.

"You leave everything to me, Miss Aleta," he had said. "I'll get these young lads into shape and we'll have no trouble with them as we might with them cockneys. I never did care for the footmen we had in London."

This was a reference back to Aleta's grandfather's time, when there had been Wayte House in Curzon Street, which had been sold years ago as premises for a Club.

"I see you are ready to receive Mr. Wardolf and his party," Aleta said to the footmen as she reached the bottom of the stairs.

"Tha' roight, Miss," one of them answered.

"Now don't forget, whatever you do, that you must never refer to me or Mr. Harry by our real names. We are Mr. and Miss Dunstan, if anyone asks you. But it would be best not to mention us at all unless you have to."

"We understands, Miss," the footmen said, almost as a chorus, and Aleta went on up the stairs.

They had talked over for ages what name they should use, most of the names seeming either too common for Aleta's liking, or too fussy for Harry's.

Finally they agreed to pick out the first name that they found in a book and hope it was appropriate.

It had been Dunstan.

"That will do," Harry said. "It sounds middle-class, which we are supposed to be."

Aleta laughed.

"You certainly don't look it."

She thought that Harry looked not only aristo-cratic but also exceedingly handsome, especially in his riding-clothes, with his boots polished under Bar-low's supervision until, as she said, she could see her face in them.

Because she was so tired she climbed very slowly up the steep, narrow stairs which led from the first floor to the second, and the second to the third.

The Nurseries looked quite attractive with pieces of furniture brought up from down below and some new curtains and covers for the chairs, which Captain Cosgrove had insisted on supplying for them.

"If you are uncomfortable," he said to Aleta when she protested, "you won't be able to do your job well, and that would be disastrous from all our points of view."

She felt a little guilty at taking anything for themselves, but the bright chintz which hung on each side of the windows and which covered the two com-fortable arm-chairs and the small sofa made the room seem very inviting.

Because she thought it would cheer up both her and Harry, Aleta had arranged a big bowl of roses on the table which had a new table-cloth, and another vase in a corner of the room was filled with blue delphiniums.

"Quite a home away from home," Aleta said mockingly as she entered it. "And now, Miss Dunstan, remember that you are employed to be efficient, and it is something you have to be."

As she spoke aloud she walked across the room to one of the windows which looked out over the front of the house.

For a moment she could see only the glimmer of gold on the lake in the afternoon sun, and as always it carried her mind away to the fairy-stories she had loved as a child.

Then she realised that coming down the drive was a large car followed by half-a-dozen others.

"They are arriving!" she exclaimed, and wondered apprehensively if Harry had had time to move himself and the half-empty bottle of champagne out of the Drawing-Room.

Then she was sure he had done so, and stood watching a little nervously as the cavalcade crossed the bridge and drove into the courtyard beneath her.

"Mr. Wardolf is certainly arriving in style!" she told herself.

Just for a moment she felt an irrepressible resentment that he should be so rich and an American; then she told herself that she was being childish.

"We are grateful to him, very grateful!" she said severely. "He is benefitting us and everyone on the Estate, and people like old Barlow and Mrs. Abbott are going to have better wages than they have ever had in the whole of their lives."

By craning her neck forward she could see that the first car had drawn up outside the front door.

Two of the footmen had already reached the car. One had opened the door and the other was standing ready to help the passengers out.

It was a woman who got out first, and Aleta, although she could only see the top of her head, realised that she was thin and elegant, and she thought this must be Mr. Wardolf's daughter, the one who was to marry a Duke.

"What's her name?" she had asked Charles Cosgrove.

"Lucy-May," he had replied.

"Two names?"

"No, they are hyphenated."

"That's funny!"

"Americans often put two names together like that," Charles Cosgrove explained. "It usually means that Momma wanted one name, and Poppa another, so they compromised by joining the two together."

Aleta laughed.

"And supposing the Godparents have other ideas?"

"Then they incorporate them in some way or another," Charles Cosgrove said. "They love names, and Mr. Wardolf's are typical. He is Cornelius Fiske Wardolf, Junior."

"Junior?" Aleta questioned.

"His father would also have been called Cornelius, so he became Cornelius Wardolf, Junior, which, strangely enough, he will doubtless continue to call himself even when his father is dead."

"It sounds very complicated."

"Not half as complicated as they find our titles."

"That I can understand," Aleta replied. "When the head of the family has one name, his first son another, and his other sons a third, it must drive them nearly crazy!"

"It does!" Captain Cosgrove agreed gravely, and it was impossible for her not to laugh.

'That will be Lucy-May,' she thought now.

Then she saw that the girl was followed from the car by a tall man with grey hair.

He was carrying his hat in his left hand, and now with his right he solemnly shook hands with both the footmen.

Aleta gave a little gurgle of laughter.

She knew how surprised the footmen would be, for this was something they certainly would not have expected.

Then the first car was driving away and it seemed as if a whole army of young people were descending from the others.

Because she was so interested, she opened the window, and as she did so, she could hear their high-pitched voices chattering as they ran up the steps and into the house.

They had expected a large party, and certainly a large party had arrived.

Aleta began to worry if everything was in order and nothing had been forgotten. Then she told herself that if there was, there was nothing she could do about it now.

She would just have to sit and wait until the problems, if there were any, were brought to her.

* * *

Riding back over the Park, Harry thought with satisfaction that so far everything seemed to have gone well.

He had decided with Charles Cosgrove that it would be quite safe for him to describe himself as the Manager of the Estate and for Mr. Wardolf to be told that anything he wanted outside the house itself should be ordered through him.

Cornelius Wardolf had therefore sent for him within an hour of his arrival at Kings Wayte.

"I wanta shake you by the hand, Mr. Dunstan," he had said, "and tell you how delighted I am with this magnificent mansion that's been procured for me by Captain Charles Cosgrove."

"I'm glad you are pleased, Sir," Harry had replied.

"Captain Cosgrove gave me a short summary of its history," Mr. Wardolf had said, "and he told me to ask you anything I wished to know about it, so I hope that when we have time you'll relate all you know on the subject."

"I'll do my best," Harry had replied, wondering how he could condense nearly four centuries of history.

"Now, I want you to tell me what's been arranged for the amusement of my guests," Mr. Wardolf went on.

He sat down as he spoke, and added:

"Take a seat, young man, and smoke, if you like. We won't stand on ceremony, you and I, considering we've gotta work together."

"Thank you, Sir," Harry said.

He liked what he saw of the American, with his grey hair and slim figure, and he guessed him to be about fifty. Also, he had a kind of aura about him which Harry recognised as belonging to a man who knew where he was going in life and allowed no obstacle to stand in his way.

He told him briefly about the horses and the cars that were waiting in the stables.

Mr. Wardolf listened, then asked sharply:

"Ball-Room?"

For a moment Harry did not understand, then he asked:

"Do you mean have we got one? Yes, certainly. There is a large Ball-Room, and the floor has recently been polished and everything is in order."

"That's great!" Mr. Wardolf said. "We'll give a Ball in the next few days. Where can I get a list of the local people who should be invited?"

Harry looked surprised.

"You intend to ask your neighbours, Sir?"

"Why not? It's the best way of getting to know them."

Harry hesitated for a moment.

He knew the County families would think it odd that a stranger to the district should invite them to the house before they themselves had called on him.

Then he told himself that perhaps he was being old-fashioned. He was quite certain that the young, at any rate, would be only too delighted that there was to be a Ball at Kings Wayte, and the lack of ceremony would certainly not deter them from attending.

"I'll let you have a list tomorrow morning, Sir," he said aloud.

"Thanks. And I suppose you can arrange for someone to send out the invitations?"

Harry thought quickly that Aleta could do that, and he nodded.

"Good! Good!" Mr. Wardolf said. "I'll want a Band, the very best, so you'd better get that from London, and if the cooks can't cope with the supper, get caterers to do it."

"You mean me to arrange it, Sir?"

"Of course! My secretary should be here in a day or two, but he's got some business arrangements to attend to in London before he can join me. But you can see to everything in the meantime."

"Very good, Sir."

This was something Harry had not expected and he thought Cosgrove should have let him know. But there was nothing he could do but agree, and when he had gone upstairs to tell Aleta what was expected, she merely smiled.

"At least he's not complaining about the comforts of the house," she had said. "And think of a Ball here at Kings Wayte! How wonderful! It's what I've always longed to see."

"It's something you won't see," Harry had said quickly. "We must both be very careful not to be seen by the neighbours, or they'll spill the beans as to who we are."

"Yes, of course, I realise that," Aleta said. "But it would be fun to dance in the Ball-Room, where there hasn't been a party, according to Mrs. Abbott, since before I was born."

"Father and Mother could not have afforded to give a Ball in their day," Harry said, "although I remember they had a lot of dinner-parties."

"That's different," Aleta said. "A Ball is something very special."

She found herself thinking of the first one she had ever attended, the Ball in Berkeley Square, and the women dancing in their ankle-length dresses draped over the hips.

Now the dresses were shorter and she had learnt from Charles Cosgrove that there were new dances.

'It's lucky I'm not going,' she thought to herself. 'I should be sadly out-of-date.'

She wondered if the man she had talked to in the Temple in Berkeley Square was dancing every night in London and if he ever thought of her as she thought of him.

Perhaps after he had left her he had never given her another thought even though he had kissed her.

Aleta felt a little thrill go through her.

Even after two years she could still feel the wonder of that kiss and remember how it had seemed to lift her up into the stars so that she had become part of the beauty of the night when she had heard the song of the nightingales.

Harry put his arm round her.

"You're looking wistful," he said. "I know you'd like to go to the Ball. Of course I wish you could, but as you well know, it is impossible."

"Of course it is," Aleta said, "but it will be fun to hear the music and know that Kings Wayte is entertaining as it used to do."

"You must keep well out of the way," Harry said firmly, as if he thought she had forgotten. "And that reminds me, you have to sit down and make a list of all the local people whom Wardolf should invite. I suppose you can remember them? I've been away so long I've almost forgotten the names of the people we used to know."

"A lot of them have moved," Aleta said, "or were killed in the war."

As she spoke, she was thinking of the children who had come to parties at Kings Wayte and whose parties she had driven to with her mother.

It had been so exciting, travelling in the closed brougham with a woollen shawl over her party-dress and her hair tied up with two bows, one over each ear.

As she thought of it she could hear the horses' hoofs as they travelled through the narrow lanes, then

up a long drive to where there was a huge house
with all its windows ablaze with light.

Inside she would find all the children whom she
had known ever since she was tiny. They would play
Musical Chairs and Oranges and Lemons, and sometimes there would be a cotillion with favours which
the boys were too shy to present, and afterwards a
large tea with jellies to eat and crackers to pull.

Then there would be the drive home, when she
would often fall asleep with her mother's arm round
her.

'The girls may be there still,' she thought, 'but
many of the boys will have lost their lives in
Flanders.'

Or some of them, like their nearest neighbour,
would be crippled from their wounds, so it might
be tactless to invite them.

A thought suddenly came to her.

"It is not only I who cannot go to the Ball,
Harry," she said, "but neither can you, and you are
such a beautiful dancer."

"We'll dance together up here," Harry said. "Or
better still, we'll dance in one of the rooms that are
not being used where we can hear the music."

Aleta clapped her hands together.

"Oh, Harry, you are wonderful! I'd love that,
and no-one could have a more handsome partner. But
you'll have to teach me to Shimmy."

Harry groaned.

"I'm not certain if I'm very good at it myself."

"But you *have* danced it?"

"Yes, of course, although I prefer to Foxtrot."

"I'm sure Mr. Wardolf's guests are very, very
up-to-date. I wish we could watch them dancing,
then we'd know how to do it."

"Now, Aleta," Harry said warningly. "No peep-
ing, no prying! You know as well as I do it's not
worth risking being exposed."

"No, of course not," Aleta agreed. "I'm only teasing. Besides, even if I were asked to the Ball, like
Cinderella I have nothing to wear."

"That's the best thing I've heard," Harry said, "because I know that in those circumstances nothing could tempt you to appear."

He was mocking her and Aleta threw a cushion at him.

He caught it and threw it back and she put it back tidily on the chair.

"You are not to spoil anything," she said. "All these new things have to last us a very long time, unless of course you marry an heiress like Lucy-May."

Harry laughed.

"I admit to having thought of that myself, but I'm too late."

"Why too late?"

"She's already got her Duke. Mr. Wardolf told me just now."

"What did he say?"

"He said: 'I want you to make quite sure, young man, that the Duke of Stadhampton, when he arrives tomorrow, is properly looked after. I guess your servants know how to treat a Duke? Make sure that he is accorded every courtesy and has everything he requires.'

" 'I'll speak to the Butler, Sir, and also to the Housekeeper to make certain His Grace will have no complaints.'

" 'He comes of a very old family, I believe?' Mr. Wardolf said.

" 'Yes, indeed, Sir. The Stadhamptons are one of the oldest families in England.'

" 'So I was told,' Mr. Wardolf said. 'I'm glad to hear you confirm it. I want him to marry my daughter.'

" 'That would be very satisfactory for you, Sir,' I replied."

When he repeated the conversation to Aleta, she laughed.

"Did he really talk in that pompous manner? He must be really impressed by the Duke."

"He is," Harry agreed. "So I have not even a chance of entering that competition."

"What does she look like?"

"I haven't seen her yet. I expect she's like all American girls—hearty, rather brash, and longing to see herself in a coronet. Dukes are a very desirable commodity at the moment in the eyes of Americans, the English taking precedence over the French."

Aleta laughed again.

"You make it sound as if they are something in a shop-window."

"That's exactly what they are," Harry said, "and they price themselves accordingly. I was told the other day what the Vanderbilts settled on their daughter who married the Duke of Marlborough. I've forgotten exactly how much, but it was something astronomical!"

Aleta made a little grimace.

"I think it's degrading to sell your title—or to sell yourself for one."

"Well, it's something which will not happen to me or you, Aleta," Harry said, "and if you want the truth, I have no desire, poor though I am, to have a rich wife who would keep reminding me that it was her money whenever I bought something I wanted."

"I certainly can't imagine that happening to you," Aleta said. "At the same time, for her sake, I hope whomever you marry has enough to buy herself a few dresses."

"That would be different," Harry said loftily. "It's a good thing for a woman to have her own pin-money. But anything more would make me feel humiliated, which is something I have no intention of feeling."

"No, of course not," Aleta agreed, "but I am certain of one thing, Harry—any woman you love will love you for yourself. You are the nicest man I have ever met in my life!"

She kissed her brother on the cheek as she spoke, and he moved away in a rather embarrassed manner.

"I had better go downstairs," he said, "and see
that everything's all right, although I'm sure Barlow
is coping admirably."

"I'm sure he is," Aleta said, "and so will Mrs.
Abbott. I shall go along to her room a little later
to hear all the gossip. She'll be able to tell me what
Lucy-May is really like. Mrs. Abbott's a good judge
of women."

"As Barlow is of men," Harry returned. "He
keeps telling me what a 'perfect gentleman' Grandfather was, and I have a feeling he doesn't think of
me that way."

Aleta had laughed, and Harry was thinking of
her laughter now as he rode his horse a little slower.

She had been wonderful over everything, he told
himself, and if she had not co-operated he would
not at this moment be riding one of the finest mounts
he had had for years, a horse he would give his
back teeth to own himself.

He rode still slower because he did not wish to
get back to the stables, where he was certain there
would be a host of things waiting for his attention.

Because he was posing as the Manager, he had
taken over the Estate Office, which was on the ground
floor of the house in the East Wing and which had
not been used since his grandfather's time.

His father had pensioned off the old Agent and
never replaced him, although he kept talking of doing so. Then had come the war and there had been no
money for one, and in fact there had been little for
him to do.

But the office was there with its huge filing-
boxes, maps of the Estate, and a very impressive desk.

"At least I shall look as though I am working,"
Harry had said when he had seen it, but then he had
found there was no need for pretence. He had to
work, and work hard.

'This is rather fun,' he thought to himself. 'Better
than sitting being miserable and wondering where
the next crust of bread is coming from.'

He looked across at the house and thought, as

Aleta had done, that any sacrifice was worth it if they could keep Kings Wayte in the family and belong to it as it belonged to them.

'This has been a real stroke of luck,' he thought.

His eyes travelled from the house down to the gardens where the lawns which had been like a hayfield a short while ago were now regaining some of their clipped velvet softness which had been characteristic of the garden in the past.

The irises round the lake needed cutting back, Harry noted, although they were picturesque, as were the king-cups reflected golden in the water.

Then he saw something swimming in the centre of the lake and thought it must be an otter.

It was years since he had seen one and he turned his horse down towards the water. As he did so he realised that it was not an otter but someone swimming.

He looked with surprise, and then as he reached the bank and sat watching, the head of the swimmer was raised and he saw to his astonishment that it was a woman.

She saw him, smiled, and with a few quick strokes came to the edge of the water near him.

"Hi!" she said. "Who are you?"

As she spoke she stood up and began to walk the last few steps towards the bank.

To Harry's astonishment, she was wearing a black bathing-suit without a skirt, which he thought was extremely becoming and at the same time very revealing. In fact he was a little shocked.

The woman climbed up the grass at his horse's feet and pulled a tight black bathing-cap from her head.

Her bobbed hair was curly and dark red, the colour, Harry thought, that the Venetian painters had used in innumerable paintings.

She looked up at him and realised that he was staring at her in a bemused fashion.

"I asked you who you are," she said. "I'm Lucy-May Wardolf, if you're interested."

With difficulty Harry found his voice.

"Good-morning, Miss Wardolf. I'm the Agent for the Estate—Harry Dunstan."

As he spoke he dismounted, and, quite unperturbed that she was dripping wet and her black bathing-dress was clinging to her, revealing every curve of her very attractive figure, Miss Wardolf held out her hand.

"Glad to meet you," she said. "Poppa told me there was an Agent who was looking after things in what he thought was an efficient manner. That's high praise from my father!"

"I am very gratified," Harry said. "Do you always swim in this way?"

"I've used more conventional pools," Lucy-May replied, "but they were certainly not as pretty as this one."

Harry smiled.

"It's a long time since I've seen anyone swimming here, not since I did so myself as a small boy."

He thought as he spoke that perhaps he had been indiscreet, but Lucy-May did not appear to notice.

"Then you'd better join me one day," she said. "I suggested to some of my guests that they might like to swim, but the English girls were horrified at the idea!"

Harry was not surprised and he said:

"You must find it rather cold."

"No, it's fine," Lucy-May answered. "But my towel's on the other side, so I'll have to swim back to get it."

She glanced across the lake, then said:

"I want to ride later this morning, and I'll want a decent horse."

"I'll see that one is at the front door at whatever time you say," Harry answered. "Will someone be escorting you?"

"I expect so, or you can join me, if you like. I can see you're a fine rider."

"Thank you," Harry said.

"No—I mean that. I saw you coming through the Park and thought you were riding differently from a lot of men who prance up and down the Rotten Road, or whatever that place in Hyde Park is called."

"Rotten Row!" Harry corrected.

"Well, they're not what I call horsemen," Lucy-May said, "and I don't think they'd fit in at Poppa's Ranch."

"Your father has a Ranch?"

"Several," Lucy-May said. "The one I like going to best is where we've got the best horses. Give me something spirited this morning. I don't want to kick an old mule along."

She smiled at him, then without saying any more she pulled on her bathing-cap and threw herself back into the water.

She swam over-arm in a way that Harry had never seen a woman swim before.

Then he thought that by staring at her perhaps he was being impertinent, and he rode away, feeling somewhat bewildered and at the same time rather intrigued.

Lucy-May Wardolf was very different from what he had expected!

he was to marry off his daughter . . . . . pity you're not . . . a Marquess or an Earl then he might have settled for you!"

Harry paused when he said:

"I felt like punching him . . . .

Chapter Three

Mr. Wardolf looked with satisfaction at his daughter as she came into the room.

She was wearing fringed suede Mexican Chaps like those she wore on his Ranch in California, a green shirt which accentuated the red of her hair, and black boots with large gold spurs.

He thought, as he had so often before, that he was lucky to have a daughter who not only had a great deal of his vitality and "go" in her but was also extremely pretty.

"I presume you're going riding?" he said.

"Yes, Pop, why don't you come with me?"

"I'm too busy getting to know this house," he replied. "At the moment it seems rather like a maze and I keep losing myself in uncharted corridors."

Lucy-May laughed.

"What you're really thinking is that you'd like to show it to some of our friends back home and see them go green with envy."

"The thought had crossed my mind," her father replied.

"Well, I'm going to explore outside, and I hope that your Manager, or whatever he calls himself, has found me a horse worth riding."

"There should be one. I paid enough for them."

"He rides well himself, so he ought to be a good judge," Lucy-May said reflectively, as if she spoke to herself.

48

"Now you leave young Dunstan alone," her father admonished, "and concentrate on the Duke. Has he come up to scratch?"

"If by that you mean has he asked me in so many words to marry him," Lucy-May replied, "the answer is no. But from the way you briefed him I imagine the whole thing is a foregone conclusion."

As she spoke, she thought that her father seemed to relax, and there was a smile on his face as he said:

"I want to see you a Duchess. It means a lot over here, and a great deal more in New York."

"I fancy the strawberry leaves will become me," Lucy-May said. "At the same time, I've got to live with the Duke—not you."

"Hampton's a very decent fellow, and far more intelligent than the average young Englishmen I've met."

"Don't forget his name is Stadhampton now," Lucy-May said. "I suppose the servants know they should call him 'Your Grace'?"

"Are you telling me I have to instruct the English on how to address their own aristocrats?" Mr. Wardolf asked in a querulous tone. "I told Dunstan to see that he was treated right, and I'll raise hell if he isn't!"

"Now, Pop, don't work yourself up," Lucy-May said soothingly. "Tybalt Stadhampton is no different from what he was when you picked him up at a party in New York and gave him a job for which he was sincerely grateful."

"So he ought to be! It's not every man, especially an Englishman, that I'd trust in my business," Mr. Wardolf said almost truculently.

"It paid dividends on this occasion," Lucy-May said with a smile, "and if he's not impressed by Kings Wayte, he ought to be! Personally, I think it's the most fascinating house I've ever seen!"

"We've got that fellow Cosgrove to thank for that," her father replied, "and a pretty penny it cost me!"

"And worth every cent of it," Lucy-May said

lightly. "Well, if you won't join me, I'll have to go on my own."

"I suppose someone is going with you?" her father asked sharply.

"Your Mr. Dunstan is," Lucy-May said over her shoulder.

She was halfway out the door when her father shouted:

"What's happened to all your friends?"

"They're dancing," Lucy-May replied.

As it happened, Harry asked the same thing as soon as their two horses, which had pranced round skittishly before they could get off, allowed them to speak.

"I should have thought your friends would have wished to accompany you," he said.

He spoke almost absent-mindedly, for his eyes were on Lucy-May's slim figure, thinking he had never seen such an extraordinary riding get-up before, but he had to admit it was exceptionally becoming.

The green open-neck blouse revealed her white skin, and she wore no hat, but what really astounded him, more than her one-piece bathing-dress had, was that she rode astride.

When Harry had left England in the war, the only women he had seen wearing trousers of any sort were girls in the munition factories, who, as a concession to feminine modesty, wore long coats of the same material over them and frilled caps to protect their hair.

He had never imagined he would escort a lady who rode astride, but he had to admit that Lucy-May rode exceptionally well, and his apprehension that the horse he had chosen for her might be too much for her to hold was groundless.

They had galloped to take some of the freshness out of their mounts, and now they slowed to an easier pace, moving side by side.

"Was this your choice?" Lucy-May asked, and he knew she was referring to her horse.

"It was," he replied briefly.

"Then I congratulate you on a good buy, whatever the actual cost."

"I hoped you would say that, and there are several others in the stables just as good."

"Then I shall certainly enjoy myself at Kings Wayte."

"Didn't you expect to?"

"I wasn't certain. I've always been told how stuffy and conventional the British are."

"We changed quite considerably during the war, and you will find, as your father's daughter, that people will be quite prepared to accept you as you are."

He spoke drily, resenting for a moment the fact that any young woman should be so rich and so sure of herself.

With a perception he had not expected, Lucy-May knew what he was thinking.

"Stop being envious!" she said sharply. "If we Americans can't have blue blood and centuries of history, we have to have something—that's only fair!"

Because she had read his thoughts Harry felt rather embarrassed. Then he said:

"I'm not really envious of you. It's just that the whole structure of the world at the moment is a little unbalanced, and I find it hard to be complacent at having to hold out the 'begging bowl.'"

"Is that what you're doing?" Lucy-May asked. "Well, I refuse to be sorry for you at the moment, when what you should really be saying is that you're enjoying yourself riding with me in very pleasant surroundings."

Harry threw back his head and laughed.

"Do you always instruct your young men on how to pay you compliments?" he asked.

"Certainly, when they are as slow as you are!"

He laughed again.

"What do you want me to say, considering that you have shocked me twice already today and I am not certain this isn't the third time?"

"Shocked you?"

Lucy-May looked at him in surprise from under her long dark eye-lashes.

"I know what you are referring to," she said suddenly, "my bathing-dress, my riding-clothes, and now of course my frankness."

She saw by Harry's expression that her guess was right and she gave a little chuckle.

"Remind me when we meet in the evening to simper behind my fan."

"You're quite safe," he replied. "That's one time we won't meet."

"Why not?"

"Because I'm in charge of the Estate. The outside workers don't come inside and vice versa."

"English rules?"

"Of course!"

"Then we shall have to see if we can break them. I presume it can be done?"

"That is something you'll never know."

"Are you prepared to bet on that?"

"No. I am merely stating a fact. You must learn, Miss Wardolf, that in England the classes keep their place."

"And what class are you?"

"I am, to all intents and purposes, your father's employee, since I manage this Estate, of which he is the tenant, on behalf of its owner."

"Who is its owner?"

"A gentleman by the name of Sir Harry Wayte."

"Will I get to meet him?"

"It's very unlikely."

"I think I'd like to meet him. He must know he's fortunate to own such a magnificent house."

"Which he can't afford!"

"So that's why he has to let it?"

"Exactly!"

"I must say there are quite a lot of things that want doing to it, the chief amongst them being the installation of some bathrooms. The English must be a very dirty race."

"Perhaps the Americans are over-clean!" Harry

flashed. "Extensive washing can be attributed to a desire to ease a guilty conscience."

"Now you are either teasing me or being impertinent," Lucy-May said, "and let me inform you, Mr. Dunstan, that my conscience is pleasantly relaxed and has no inhibitions of any sort."

"How many extra bathrooms do you want?" Harry enquired.

"I should think about a dozen would do to start with," Lucy-May replied.

"You are joking!"

"No. As a matter of fact I was discussing it with Poppa this morning, and he'll be giving you orders to get them installed right away."

For a moment Harry was speechless.

He wanted to say that such an idea was ridiculous and unnecessary, considering that they had taken the house for only a year.

Then it suddenly struck him that Cosgrove had been right in saying the extra benefits from letting the house would be just as important as the rent, astronomical as it was.

He began to see what a tremendous advantage it would be to have the right plumbing installed all over Kings Wayte, new bathrooms and, he thought, basins in the Powder-Rooms which were attached to many of the State Bedrooms.

It would save the water being carried up the long stairs from the kitchen by servants who, growing old, found it more and more difficult.

It would save long walks down draughty corridors in the winter to the two bathrooms there were at the moment, one of which had a gas geyser which alternately refused to work at all or appeared to be in the process of blowing up.

Suddenly, for the first time, he was genuinely glad that the Wardolfs had come to Kings Wayte.

Although he had tried to repress it, he had still been feeling a little resentment that his house should be invaded by strangers who, however much they paid him, were still alien to the English way of life and foreigners as far as he and Aleta were concerned.

He realised that Lucy-May was waiting for him to speak, and with a smile that illuminated his face and made him look extremely handsome he said:

"You shall have your bathrooms, Miss Wardolf, just as quickly as I can supply them, and to celebrate I'll race you to the end of this field!"

* * *

Aleta walked down the backstairs to the House-keeper's room, where she knew she would find Mrs. Abbott.

Sure enough, the old woman was sitting in a comfortable arm-chair, a cup of tea in her hand and her feet up on a stool in front of the fire.

"Don't move, Abby," Aleta said quickly. "I want to talk to you, but you must rest whenever you have the chance."

"It doesn't seem right, Miss Aleta," Mrs. Abbott replied, "but to tell the truth, my legs kept me awake half the night; aching terrible they were."

"That's why you must put them up when you get the chance," Aleta said, "and do try to save yourself from going up and down the stairs. I'm sure Rose is beginning to understand what's required."

"They're all doing their best, Miss," Mrs. Abbott replied, "but though these young girls are willing enough, you 'can't make a silk purse out of a sow's ear,' as my old mother used to say."

"They will learn," Aleta said confidently, "and I can't believe the young ladies in this party are half as fastidious or demanding as the ladies who were our guests in Grandpapa's time."

"No indeed, Miss. And their dresses are nothing like the same, either. Would you believe..." Mrs. Abbott lowered her voice as she added in a shocked tone: "they wear very little underneath—very little indeed!"

Aleta smiled to herself, but aloud she said:

"That saves extra work, and I imagine, from the

sound of the Gramophone drifting up the stairs, that they're quite happy dancing."

"Dancing!" Mrs. Abbott snorted. "That's all they ever do! Dancing after breakfast they were this morning! Did you ever hear anything like it? Her Ladyship would never have believed it possible!"

Aleta knew that the reference to Her Ladyship was not to her mother but to her grandmother, for Mrs. Abbott lived very much in the past, in the days when she ruled the inside of the great house with a rod of iron and everything was done in the same way as at Woburn, Chatsworth, or Knowle.

In fact, Mrs. Abbott's proud boast in the past had always been that the guests at Kings Wayte said they were more comfortable there than at any other house at which they had stayed.

"As long as everyone's happy, I don't think anything else matters," Aleta said aloud.

"New clothes or not," Mrs. Abbott said sharply, "the young ladies leave their rooms looking like pigsties! Things thrown about everywhere, and would you believe it, Miss, face-powder scattered all over the dressing-tables!"

This had obviously shocked Mrs. Abbott even more than the lack of underclothes, and Aleta said soothingly:

"When I was in London I found that all the girls wore face-powder and lipstick."

Mrs. Abbott held up her hands in horror.

"I don't know what the world's coming to, Miss, that I don't! I can tell you, a lady who used lipstick before the war was considered no better than she should be!"

Aleta was aware that this was the final condemnation, and to change the subject she said:

"It will be exciting to have a Ball here again. It will seem just like old times."

"That's what I thought when I hears about it," Mrs. Abbott said, "but I suppose you know already, Miss, that they're thinking of engaging a black Band!"

This was obviously so horrifying that the House-keeper's voice was hardly above a whisper.

"They're very popular in London," Aleta said quickly.

"A black Band at Kings Wayte is something I never expected to see in all me born days!" Mrs. Abbott said firmly.

This was obviously a dangerous subject and Aleta decided not to pursue it.

"I shall listen to the music and wish I could go to the Ball myself," she said. "And do you know, I think I shall be able to watch, although Sir Harry said I couldn't do so."

"Watch, Miss? How is that possible?" Mrs. Abbott enquired.

"Well, the Band is very unlikely to sit in the Musicians Gallery as they did in the old days," Aleta said. "Everything is very intimate now and Bands are always on the same level as the dancers. So I shall be able to creep into the Musicians Gallery and see everyone dancing beneath me."

"Now you be careful, Miss," Mrs. Abbott said. "You don't want anyone recognising you."

"There are only a few people coming who would," Aleta said.

She spoke a little wistfully and Mrs. Abbott said quickly:

"When this is all over, Miss, and these Americans have gone away, you and Master Harry can have some parties of your own—not a Ball, perhaps, but your friends in for dinner."

"Yes, of course," Aleta agreed, "and that'll be very exciting. Now I must leave you to have a rest. Is there anything that is wanted?"

Mrs. Abbott, as if she had waited for this cue, went through a long recitation of how stupid several of the girls from the village had been, and how she had shown them a dozen times how to turn down the beds properly and lay out the ladies' nightgowns.

She was also indignant because the footmen had

spilt some water they were bringing upstairs for those
who bathed in their own bedrooms.

While the gentlemen who had stayed at Kings
Wayte in the past had used the bathrooms, inadequate
though they were, the ladies had always used hip-
baths in front of their bedroom fires.

In fact, Aleta knew that her mother would have
been horrified at the idea of walking about the corridors in her dressing-gown, and both she and her
grandmother would have thought it an impossible
idea for either of them to use a communal bath.

Things had changed, Aleta knew, with the war,
and she and her Governess had had to cope with
the unpredictable geyser for the simple reason that
there was no-one left in the house who was capable
of carrying heavy cans of hot water up the stairs.

She was thinking that it was nice to have young
housemaids and footmen to wait on them again, when
she heard Mrs. Abbott say something about "His
Grace" and listened more attentively.

"Fussin', the American gentleman was, over
whether the Queen's Room was good enough for
His Grace," the old Housekeeper was saying. "I felt
like saying to him: 'If 'twas good enough for Queen
Anne, it's good enough for any modern Duke!' But
there, these Americans don't understand, do they,
Miss?"

"Mr. Wardolf is very anxious that the Duke
should enjoy himself," Aleta said, "because he is to
marry Miss Lucy-May."

"That's what I heard," Mrs. Abbott said, "and if
you ask me, Miss, it's a pity a nobleman like His
Grace has to sell himself, so to speak, just to keep
things going."

Aleta was surprised at Mrs. Abbott's knowledge
of the situation. Then she remembered that nothing
could ever be kept from the servants.

"I expect the Duke is as hard-up as we are,"
she said quietly.

"I'm praying that Master Harry doesn't have to

marry an American," Mrs. Abbott said sharply. "Their money's all right, but if you ask me, Miss, they don't know how to behave, not like us."

Aleta repressed a smile and said:

"Their way of life is of course different from ours, Mrs. Abbott, but whether they are American, French, or even German, they are still people."

"Them Germans!" Mrs. Abbott sniffed. "They're not people, they're beasts in human form, that's what I thinks."

Aleta knew this was a hobby-horse, and, rising from the chair on which she had been sitting, she said:

"While everyone's dancing downstairs I'll slip along and see that the rooms are all right, so you need not bother. Promise me you'll stay here and rest, and perhaps have a nap."

"You're very kind, Miss Aleta," Mrs. Abbott said, "and I do feel a bit tired."

"Then I'll see to everything," Aleta said, "and report back later."

She left the Housekeeper's room and went along the passage and through the green baize door that led to the main part of the house.

Here the music from downstairs was very loud and she recognised the tune they were playing.

It was "I'm Just Wild About Harry" and she thought how appropriate it was to the household even though no-one else realised it.

She began to hum to herself as she walked along the corridor which led to the State Bedrooms, which had been repaired and redecorated first.

There was still a lot to be done, but nevertheless with a quick coat of paint and new curtains they looked very different from the drab, dusty, dilapidated rooms that had so horrified Harry when he returned from France.

Aleta peeped into several to find that they had been left tidy by the house-maids and, as she had instructed, there was a vase of flowers on each dressing-table.

Then she reached the Queen's Room and as she opened the door it made her think of her mother.

The King's Room, in which her father had slept, and the Queen's Room formed a Suite of their own, and she had supposed that Lucy-May would occupy what was known as the Queen's Room while her father would be in the Master Bedroom.

But Mr. Wardolf had made it very clear that after his own room the Duke of Stadhampton was to have the next best, and that must be the room which had been occupied by Queen Anne when she made a State Visit to Kings Wayte in 1710.

It was a large room with a four-poster bed draped with finely embroidered curtains, and with a ceiling rioting with gods and goddesses, which had been much improved by a hasty cleaning.

It was a room that Aleta had always loved and she felt as if her mother's presence was still there, so that she found herself thinking that even the fragrance of the roses which stood on a beautifully inlaid chest-of-drawers was somehow redolent of her childhood.

Whatever else in the house had been sold, Aleta had been determined that nothing should be taken from this room.

Now her eyes went appreciatively to the French furniture with its chased gold handles, the carved gilt mirrors, and the Dresden china which decorated the mantelpiece.

'At least the Duke will appreciate what this room contains,' she thought, and tried to remember what she knew about his house.

His was a familiar name, but she had never heard him spoken about either by her friends or by Harry, although they had often talked of the wonders of Chatsworth, and when she had been in London the Duke and Duchess of Devonshire had invited her Godmother and her to a dance at Devonshire House.

Aleta had been unable to go because the day before the Ball was to take place she had learnt of her father's illness and had rushed back to Kings Wayte.

After that she had never left it again, but she sometimes regretted not seeing more of London and its great houses, which were slowly beginning to re-open after the war but, she was told, with much of their grandeur diminished or lost.

'Perhaps the Duke is in the same position as we are,' she thought.

Then she was sure that that was the reason why he was coming to stay at Kings Wayte.

It was to marry in order to save his house and his Estate as perhaps eventually Harry might have to do, because once their rich tenants had left they would be facing the same problems they had faced before.

"Always money, money, money!" Aleta said to herself miserably.

With a last glance round the room she returned to the corridor and started to walk back the way she had come.

She had just reached the landing overlooking the marble Hall, and was hurrying in case anyone should see her before she reached the safety of the baize door which led into the servants' quarters, when she heard a car drive up to the front door.

Because she was curious, she instinctively moved to the landing to see who it might be.

Then as the footman on duty went down to greet the newcomer she heard a man's voice say sharply:

"I've got to speak to Mr. Wardolf, and quickly! There's been an accident!"

Aleta stood still.

It sprang to her mind that something had happened to Harry. She saw Barlow come into the Hall and walk without hurrying towards the rather tough-looking man who was just coming through the front door.

"Did I hear you say there's been an accident,

Sir?" he enquired, his voice calm and respectfully modulated.

"Yes, you did," the newcomer answered, "and to one of Mr. Wardolf's guests. There were two gentlemen in the car, but 'twas a Duke, I understands, as was hurt."

"I very much regret to hear that," Barlow said, "and I know Mr. Wardolf will be deeply distressed. If you will wait a moment, Sir, I'll inform him of your arrival."

By now Aleta could see the man who had come in the car, and she realised from his clothes and his accent that he was a farmer or a countryman of some sort.

She knew that Barlow had already sized him up and, because he was not a gentleman, was prepared to leave him standing in the Hall while he went away in search of Mr. Wardolf.

One of the footmen asked:

"Was it a bad accident, Sir?"

Excited by what had occurred and only too ready to be garrulous, the farmer replied:

"Going too fast, they were, but young men never do anything else. They rounds the corner in Marsh Lane and would've collided head on with a farm-waggon if the driver had not turned the car into the hedge."

"The hedge!" one of the footmen ejaculated.

"That wouldn't have mattered, except he struck a tree, so that the gentleman in the passenger-seat banged his head against the wind-screen. You couldn't expect anythin' else."

"No, of course not," the footman agreed. "What sort of car was it, Sir?"

"Car?" the farmer repeated, scratching his head. "One of them new-fangled ones, as travels far too fast for my liking. I knows—it were a Bentley!"

"A Bentley!" the footman repeated, obviously impressed.

He was just about to ask some more questions when Barlow returned with Mr. Wardolf.

"What's this? What's happened?" the American asked. "An accident to the Duke? How could such a thing have happened?"

The farmer explained all over again what had occurred, while Mr. Wardolf fired staccato questions at him.

Then he asked:

"Where is the Duke? What's happened to him?"

"They're bringing him here, Sir, on the hay-cart. They thought it'd be too bumpy in my little bus."

"Quite right! Quite right!" Mr. Wardolf said. "A Doctor! We need a Doctor!"

"Dr. Goodwin's on holiday, Sir, but there's a stranger taking his place until he returns."

"A Doctor?"

"Oh, yes, Sir. I believes so."

"Then fetch him! Fetch him right away!"

"I'll do that," the farmer said.

But Mr. Wardolf was not listening, he was giving orders.

"Tell the Housekeeper to see that the Duke's room is ready for him, and have bandages and whatever else he's likely to require ready. Do you understand?"

"Yes, Sir."

One of the footmen came hurrying up the front stairs and Aleta met him as he turned towards the green baize door.

"It's all right, James," she said. "I heard what has happened. I'll see to everything. Just make sure that Sir Harry ... I mean Mr. Dunstan ... is told what has occurred as soon as he gets back from riding. You can leave a message for him in the stable-yard."

"I'll do that, Miss."

Aleta slipped away, hearing, as she did so, Mr. Wardolf still booming out orders in the front Hall.

'This will upset things for him,' she thought.

But she didn't feel very sorry either for the American or for the Duke who was wooing his daughter.

'They'll both have to put up with trouble and

difficulties like everyone else,' she thought, and hurried along the passage to tell Mrs. Abbott the news.

* * *

The Duke felt as if he was at the end of a long dark tunnel, but he could hear voices. What they were saying made no sense, and it was only irritating that they should have disturbed him when obviously he had been asleep.

Then a soft voice said:

"It's all right, Abby, don't fuss. The Doctor said he was unlikely to regain consciousness for at least twenty-four hours, and tomorrow a Nurse will be arriving from London."

"It's not right that you should sit up alone with a gentleman, Miss, as well you know!" an elderly voice said severely.

There was a faint little gurgle of laughter.

"If you are worrying about my not being chaperoned, Abby, I can assure you I am quite safe!"

"Your mother would not approve, Miss, as well you know!"

There was silence for a moment, then Aleta said:

"I feel that as I'm here in Mama's room she will look after me very effectively. So go to bed, Abby dear, and you can take over first thing tomorrow morning before anyone is awake."

"I don't like it, Miss. I don't like it at all!" Mrs. Abbott said.

"It's only for one night," Aleta replied patiently, "and the Doctor said someone must be with him. You know as well as I do that Ethel and Rose are too old, and the girls are all too young, so there's only me. I shall very likely doze quietly in the chair, and tomorrow when you are in charge I'll sleep just as long as you want me to."

"Well, it's not right, and that's a fact!" Mrs. Abbott said. "If you ask me, that new Doctor doesn't know his job. If only Dr. Goodwin had been here I'm certain he'd have found someone."

"But he's away," Aleta said, "so go to bed. Otherwise you'll be no use tomorrow, and you know we'll all be relying on you, expecially Mr. Wardolf. He's in a tizzy about his precious Duke."

"That's true, Miss. He couldn't have made more of a to-do if the gentleman had been the King himself! Now, I remember when King Edward..."

"Go to bed, Abby!" Aleta interrupted, knowing how interminable Mrs. Abbott's stories could be.

"Very well, Miss, but you promise you'll come and call me if there's any change in the gentleman's condition!"

"I promise," Aleta said. "Good-night, Abby."

"Good-night, Miss. I hopes as I'm doing right in leaving you."

"Go to bed!" Aleta said firmly.

Shutting the door quietly behind the Housekeeper, she walked to the side of the bed to stand looking down at the Duke.

He wondered if he should open his eyes and see what the owner of the soft voice looked like. He had not understood half of what she had said, but he had listened to her voice.

Somehow it seemed to be vaguely familiar but he was not sure. Anyway, he was too tired and was still far down the dark tunnel, although it was not as long as it had seemed at first.

Then it was too much of an effort to think and everything faded away...

* * *

The Duke awoke and heard a voice he did not recognise as his own calling out:

"Look out! Look out, you fool!"

He was struggling to put his hands in front of his face when he felt a cool hand on his forehead and heard the voice he had heard before say:

"It's all right. You are quite safe. Nothing will hurt you. Go to sleep."

He still wanted to move his hands, but he realised they were under the blankets, and the hand on his forehead was compelling.

He murmured something and thought it sounded incoherent.

"You've had an accident," the soft voice said, "but not a very bad one, and you'll soon be quite all right. Just sleep. You are very tired, and you'll feel better tomorrow."

The voice was almost hypnotic and he felt himself sinking down against the pillows, the tension leaving his body.

Then the voice said almost as if she spoke to herself:

"You may be thirsty."

She moved away and some moments later the Duke felt her lift his head and hold a glass to his lips.

Automatically he swallowed what was tipped into his mouth and knew it was lemonade.

It took away a dryness that he had not realised was there. Then very gently his head was set down against the pillows.

"Now go to sleep," the voice said.

He felt her hand on his forehead again, but now it was moving very gently, massaging his skin, soothing it, evoking a feeling of languor which was very pleasant.

He knew he was drifting away ... and it was like being carried on the softness of a cloud. ...

*　*　*

Aleta reached her own bedroom and started to undress.

The light was coming through the sides of the curtains and she pulled them back to look out, seeing the mist over the lake and the trees in the Park silhouetted against a pale gold sky.

She was tired, but at the same time she wondered if it would be possible to sleep.

"If I do, it must not be for long," she told herself. "I'm sure there will be a lot to do in the house this morning."

She had not been surprised when Mrs. Abbott

had come into the Queen's Room soon after five o'clock in the morning.

That was the time the staff had always risen at Kings Wayte in the old days, and although Aleta would have liked the old woman to rest a little longer, she knew it would be impossible for her to do so.

"Is everything all right, Miss?" she asked as soon as she reached Aleta's side.

"Perfectly all right, Abby," Aleta replied. "Our patient has been very quiet on the whole. He awoke once, talking nonsense, but I gave him a drink and he went back to sleep again."

"He didn't see you, Miss?"

"No. He didn't open his eyes," Aleta replied, "but even if he had, I doubt if he would have recognised anything or anybody."

"Well, thank goodness! If that new Doctor's to be believed, there'll be a real Nurse here tonight. Now you go off to bed, Miss, and have a good sleep. I'll take turns to be on duty here with Ethel and Rose until the Nurse arrives."

"Then I won't worry about anything," Aleta said with a smile.

She had, as it happened, stood at the bedside several times during the night, looking at the Duke and wondering how he could marry for money.

It was one thing to let a house as she and Harry had done to keep their heads above water, but marriage was something very different, and she knew that the more she looked at the Duke the more she despised him for not trying to save his family Estate by some other means rather than sacrificing himself.

It would be a sacrifice! No Englishman of the importance of the Duke of Stadhampton would contemplate marrying the daughter of an American millionaire for any other reason than to possess her money.

Aleta was not a snob in the way that the Social

World, before the war, had thought position and breeding more important than anything else.

But she realised that ingrained in every English man and woman of her generation was a deep respect and a pride in their antecedents and everything that they entailed.

It was King Edward who had introduced into Society men who were rich and who advised him financially. For their services to him they expected to be received socially by his friends and His Majesty had made sure that they were.

It had been, she learnt, such a revolutionary step that her grandfather and grandmother's generation had been appalled at the King's behaviour, although they were certainly not prepared to say so except secretly to their close friends.

Aleta had been told, and she believed it, that the war had broken down a great number of class barriers, and it was more her idealism than anything else which was shocked at the thought of a man like the Duke selling himself and his title to the highest bidder.

She did not blame the Americans for wishing to acquire coronets for their daughters in the same manner as they acquired paintings, furniture, and anything else which took their fancy in impoverished Europe.

What was wrong was that the owners of such treasures were over-eager to sell.

What made it worse, she thought, was that the Duke was very good-looking.

He was older than she had expected, perhaps twenty-eight or thirty, and although he was dark-haired he had a characteristically English face and could never have been mistaken for any other nationality.

She thought too, looking at him, that his broad forehead showed intelligence, and she wondered why he didn't use his brains to acquire the money he needed rather than barter for it with his title.

Then she told herself that it was none of her business, and yet looking at him when they were alone in the candlelight she thought that he presented an enigma she would like to solve.

Why did he make such a decision? How had it happened that he had no alternative except to marry an heiress?

Then she asked herself somewhat cynically if it was in fact the only alternative.

Was he not perhaps one of those men who never could have enough money? A sportsman who wished to have one of the huge covert shoots at which King Edward had been a frequent guest, or a yachtsman who wanted to race at Cowes and entertain his friends on the grouse moors of Scotland?

She remembered stories her mother had told her of the lavish hospitality that had taken place in her grandfather's day when at Kings Wayte there would often be thirty or forty guests, each of them attended by one or more personal servants.

"It must have been very expensive, Mama," Aleta remembered saying.

"It was," her mother replied with a sigh, "but your grandfather could afford it. We cannot."

"I suppose I despise you," Aleta said silently to the unconscious man lying on the bed. "And yet, if your house is as beautiful as Kings Wayte, then I suppose you feel any sacrifice is worthwhile."

She knew that Harry was right when he had said that he had no wish to marry a woman who was very much richer than himself.

A man must be master in his own house, and to feel beholden to his wife for every penny he spent would be humiliating and degrading.

"Harry and I will manage somehow," she said in her heart, still speaking silently to the man on the bed. "We may have to do all sorts of strange things, like letting this house, but we will not surrender ourselves to the financial slavery, because that is what it would be, of marrying without love, but only for gain."

Even as she thought, she remembered how many women did exactly that for a husband and a title, a place in Society. All of which she knew quite well was the ambition of every girl of her generation.

Something within her had always shrunk from the thought and she knew that she could never marry without love, however difficult it might be to remain single.

"An old maid!"

She found herself repeating the words beneath her breath and wondering if that was all that awaited her in the future.

Then she told herself that anything would be preferable, even loneliness, to marriage with a man she did not love.

She looked again at the Duke's head on the pillow.

It struck her that because he was so good-looking a lot of women must have loved him.

"Perhaps I'm wrong," she told herself. "Perhaps Lucy-May does love him, and perhaps he loves her."

It was something she wanted to believe, like making a fairy-tale come true.

Then she knew that she was only making excuses for him—excuses because he was so handsome—just like the Prince in her fairy-tale.

Chapter Four

There was a knock on the door and the Duke, who was sitting in the window with a rug over his knees, looked up.

The door opened and Lucy-May's smiling face appeared.

"Are you ready for visitors?" she asked.

"I'm delighted to see you," the Duke answered.

Lucy-May walked into the bedroom. In her hand she carried a large parcel.

"Now that you are better, I have a special present for you," she said, "with love from Poppa and of course from me."

"A present?" the Duke queried.

He was looking a little thinner after being laid up for nearly four days, but it made him perhaps even better-looking than before.

Lucy-May put the parcel down on his knees.

"Open it," she said. "I want to see if you are pleased."

The Duke pulled off the outer wrapping and found that underneath there was a painting, not a very large one, but when he looked at it he drew in his breath.

For a moment he seemed stunned into silence. Then he said:

"Is it really my Canaletto?"

"I have the pair to it downstairs," a voice said from the doorway, "and your Van Dyke."

Holding the painting in his hands, the Duke looked at Mr. Wardolf with a question in his eyes. The American walked towards him and explained:

"I bought them in London yesterday. Why didn't you tell me you were selling them?"

The Duke did not reply for a moment and Lucy-May said:

"Poppa is giving them to you. Tell him you are pleased."

"I don't know what to say," the Duke murmured.

Mr. Wardolf put his hand on his guest's shoulder.

"Say nothing, my boy. They're part of your wedding-present, and they must go back where they belong."

"Now, Poppa!" Lucy-May interposed. "I told you not to say anything like that."

"Sorry, sorry," the American said blithely, "I forgot."

"I told you not to forget," Lucy-May said positively.

There was a note of irritation in her voice which her father didn't miss.

"I suppose, like all women," he drawled, "you want a proposal of marriage with the violins playing."

"Yes, I do!" Lucy-May snapped. "With a moon overhead and nightingales singing in the trees."

She was looking angrily at her father as she spoke, so she did not see the Duke stiffen or the strange look which came into his eyes as he repeated beneath his breath:

"Nightingales!"

Then as if he was a trifle embarrassed by his daughter's anger Mr. Wardolf said:

"I have a proposition to make to you, my boy, when you are feeling fit enough to hear it."

"I am fit now," the Duke said hastily, "but I must first say I can't accept the present you have given me. It is too generous."

"It's common sense," Mr. Wardolf retorted. "I don't want to think of Hampton Castle depleted of all its treasures, and next time let me know when you are putting any of them up for sale."

The Duke's lips tightened and there was an expression on his face which Lucy-May did not understand.

"I'll leave you two together," she said blithely, "and come back later. Don't tire Tybalt, Poppa, the first day he is up. You know what the Doctor said."

"I don't think what I'm going to say will tire him," Mr. Wardolf said, seating himself in a chair opposite the Duke.

He waited until Lucy-May had left the room, then he said:

"From what I've heard, you've a very fine Castle and several other houses which contain objects of historical value."

"That's true," the Duke agreed, "but as I have only just inherited them from my uncle, everything is somewhat chaotic, which is the reason why I have not asked you to stay."

"I understand that, of course," Mr. Wardolf said. "I suppose, having been brought up with such a background, you know a great deal about paintings and such-like."

The Duke smiled.

"I like to think I do. I certainly hate to part with any of the things which are not really mine but a heritage which should be handed on to the future generations that follow me."

Mr. Wardolf nodded his head.

"That's why you must put your Canalettos and the Van Dyke back in the places where they belong."

"It is very kind of you," the Duke said, "but . . ."

"I don't want to argue about it," the American interrupted. "I just want you to listen to what I have to suggest."

The Duke put the painting down beside his chair and sat back.

"As you know," Mr. Wardolf began, "I'm hoping that you and Lucy-May, who is the most precious thing I possess, will be happy together, but I realise that although I have a very large fortune—you know it is one of the largest in America—there are things you possess which no money can buy."

The Duke was listening, and it seemed that some of the stiffness with which he had held himself when Mr. Wardolf had started speaking was gradually ebbing away and now there was a more sympathetic look in his eyes.

"I understand," the American went on, "that not only you and a great number of other English noblemen have to sell treasures which have been accumulated by your ancestors over the centuries, but the same situation exists in Europe, particularly in France."

The Duke did not speak, he merely waited, his eyes on the older man's face.

"What I am suggesting," Mr. Wardolf said, "is that as you have an ingrained knowledge of art you should acquire for me paintings and furniture which I can enjoy while I am alive, and which, when I am dead, will form the nucleus of a Gallery."

The Duke was now interested, and he bent forward.

"Do you really mean that, Sir?"

"I mean it," Mr. Wardolf said, "for I think it's important that we Americans should have a chance to appreciate the great Masters of the past."

There was a slightly cynical smile on his lips as he added:

"I'm not a fool! I've heard the things that are said about the American 'bargain-hunters,' the tales that circulate of how they have been duped by sharp Italians and crafty Frenchmen into spending enormous sums on fakes and forgeries. I don't wish to make a fool of myself in the same way."

"I can understand that," the Duke murmured.

"What I'm asking you to do is to act as my agent in Europe."

The Duke's eye-brows went up and Mr. Wardolf continued:

"I know there would be plenty of people only

too willing to oblige me in this particular, but quite frankly I would rather trust you. I like you and I have a feeling you are a better judge of paintings than half the Art Dealers who are really only interested in their own commission."

He paused before he continued:

"The commission taken by the big Art Dealers like Lord Duveen fluctuates, I understand, between twenty-five and one hundred percent on the buying price. I shall offer you fifty percent. We will make a different arrangement for my other proposition."

"What is that, Sir?" the Duke asked, his voice slightly hoarse.

"I intend to invest some money in Europe. The President has already said that the United States will help to rebuild and support European industries. I will do a little of that on my own."

"A good idea, Sir," the Duke replied.

"I will be guided entirely by your advice."

The Duke did not speak for a moment. Then he said:

"I'm honoured by your trust in me, but I'm wondering if I know enough either about art or industry."

"I've an idea that your instinct in such matters would be just as valuable as another man's acquired knowledge," Mr. Wardolf replied.

"I hope you are right," the Duke said. "At the same time, it will be a great responsibility."

"I think you'll find it'll be well worth your while."

The American knew the Duke understood that it would make him independent of any fortune brought him by his wife.

Mr. Wardolf was a shrewd enough business-man not to press a point he had already made but to leave a proposition to be assimilated, and he rose to his feet.

"I have strict instructions from Lucy-May not to tire you, but think over what I have suggested. I've a feeling it will be very interesting for you and an education for my American-minded daughter."

He left the bedroom before his guest could

speak, and when he had gone the Duke sat looking with unseeing eyes out the window.

Strangely enough, he was not thinking of what his American host had suggested to him but of something very different.

He sat almost motionless for some time before the door opened and Mrs. Abbott came in.

"I was just wondering, Your Grace, how you're feeling," she said. "The Doctor said you could stay up as long as you wanted, but if you're tired you should slip back to bed."

"I am not tired," the Duke answered, "not yet, at any rate. If you want the truth, Mrs. Abbott, I'm looking forward to tomorrow, when I can go downstairs."

"I'm sure you are, Your Grace. No gentleman likes to be an invalid for long."

"That is true," the Duke agreed. "Meanwhile, I would be grateful if you could tell me something."

"Of course, Your Grace."

Mrs. Abbott crossed her arms over her black silk apron and stood waiting respectfully.

She was thinking to herself that the Duke was not only a very nice-looking gentleman but nicely spoken and very pleasant to serve.

"What I was wondering," the Duke said slowly, as if he was choosing his words, "is who looked after me the first night after the accident. I understand from the Nurse who left this morning that she only arrived the day after I had been smashed up in the car."

"That's true, Your Grace."

"Then who was with me on the first night?"

There was a pause, as if Mrs. Abbott was thinking. Then she said:

"It's really slipped my mind, Your Grace, but I think it must have been either Rose or Ethel who was with you."

Her eyes shifted slightly as she spoke and the Duke knew she was lying.

*   *   *

Lucy-May came down the steps, and glancing across the lake she thought that the early-morning mist rising from the water made it look more attractive than at any other time.

"I might swim later," she told herself, then looked at the two horses that were waiting for her.

To her surprise, there was a groom whom she had not seen before riding the second horse.

"Where is Mr. Dunstan?" she asked.

The groom who was holding her mount replied:

"He sent Jem this mornin', Miss."

"Why?"

"Oi don't roightly know, Miss. He jest told Jem to roid wi' ye."

"And where is Mr. Dunstan now?"

"He be in th' stables, Miss."

Lucy-May mounted her horse, which was fidgety and ready to go, but rode not towards the Park but round the side of the houe towards the stables.

When she reached them she saw Harry glance in her direction, then disappear into one of the stalls.

She rode up to it and as an elderly groom came towards her, touching his forelock respectfully, she said sharply:

"Tell Mr. Dunstan I want to speak to him."

The groom walked into the stable and Lucy-May waited, tapping her boot impatiently with her riding-whip.

A few minutes later Harry came from the stable.

"Good-morning, Miss Wardolf. Is anything wrong?" he asked.

"Why are you not riding with me?"

"I'm rather busy."

"I want you to come with me as you always do."

"You'll find that Jem is a good rider."

"I'm not interested in Jem. I want you to ride with me. In fact, it is an order!"

As Lucy-May spoke she saw Harry's lips tighten, and she realised she had made a mistake.

"Please . . ." she said in a very different tone of voice. "Please come with me."

He looked up at her and she thought he was about to refuse. Then, as if he felt their conversation was embarrassing in front of the grooms, he said with a not particularly good grace:

"Very well, if that is what you wish."

As if he had anticipated what might happen, Jem had already dismounted, and Harry flung himself into the saddle. Without waiting for Lucy-May to go first, he rode down the stable-yard and out through the arched gate.

She caught him up, glanced at the somewhat grim expression on his face, and said nothing.

Only as they crossed the bridge over the lake and reached the Park did she touch her horse with the riding-whip, and the next moment they were both galloping neck-to-neck, thundering over the soft ground, chunks of turf flying out behind them.

They galloped for nearly a mile, until as they let their horses slow down a little there was a sudden spatter of rain-drops.

Harry looked up at the sky.

Rain-clouds obscured the glimmer of the sun and it seemed obvious that they were in for a storm.

He looked at Lucy-May, who, as usual, was riding bare-headed and wearing only an open-necked shirt.

"You are going to get wet," he said. "It may only be a skud, but there's a hay-barn at the end of the next field."

Lucy-May flashed him a smile, then they were off again, galloping frantically through the rain, which was getting heavier every second.

They were both breathless when they reached the old barn. It was in a somewhat dilapidated condition but nevertheless it was large and empty enough to provide shelter for them and the horses.

They went in through the open door, which had

lost one of its hinges, bending their heads as they did so.

Then Harry quickly dismounted and went to Lucy-May's side to help her from the saddle, but she slipped to the ground before he could assist her. He looked at her in consternation.

"You are wet," he said. "Here, take my coat."

He pulled off his tweed riding-jacket as he spoke.

As he did so, her horse wandered away, as Harry's own mount had done, to where in a corner of the barn there was still some hay stored from the previous year.

"I'm all right," Lucy-May said as Harry put his coat over her shoulders.

Then she looked up at him and their faces were very close to each other's.

She looked into his eyes and knew he was about to turn away. Then without really thinking she put her arm round his neck and her lips were on his.

For a moment it seemed as if Harry was frozen into immobility, before instinctively his arms went round her and for one moment he held her close and his lips possessed hers.

Then abruptly he pushed her away, the coat he had put over her shoulders falling to the ground as he did so.

"You had no right to do that!"

His voice was deep and at the same time sharp, as if he forced himself to speak harshly.

"I've wanted to do it for a long time," Lucy-May replied.

"That's why I decided we should not ride together."

"I had to see you, Harry."

"That's an absurd remark, and you know it! In the future you will ride with your friends or with the grooms, but not with me."

Another girl might have been abashed by the firm way in which Harry spoke, but Lucy-May was different.

With one step she was close to him, looking up into his face.

"Listen, Harry," she said, "I want to be with you, and I know you want to be with me. Why are you being difficult?"

"I am not being difficult but honourable," he replied. "I am your father's employee, and I shouldn't make clandestine assignations with his daughter behind his back!"

Lucy-May gave a little laugh.

"You make it sound very dashing and romantic! All I want is to be with you, Harry, and that we should ride together and talk together. You know as well as I do that it's only early in the morning that we can be alone."

"That is what we mustn't be," Harry said positively. "Leave me alone and marry your Duke! I'm not the sort of man who enjoys amorous intrigue with a woman who belongs to somebody else."

"I belong to no-one but myself," Lucy-May retorted. "As for the Duke, it was Poppa's idea that I should marry him—not mine!"

"Nevertheless you'll enjoy yourself as a Duchess," Harry said. "Think how envious all your American friends will be when you tell them you have been received at Buckingham Palace and have attended the Opening of Parliament glittering with diamonds."

There was no mistaking now the cynical sarcasm in his voice, and again Lucy-May laughed.

"Do you think that's all I want of life?" she asked. "I would enjoy having a ride with you far more than watching a King puffing about in his crown."

Harry didn't speak for a moment. Then he turned to look down at Lucy-May as he said firmly:

"Let's get this thing straight. You have your life, and I have mine."

"That's not true," Lucy-May said. "We've met, and however much you may deny it, Harry, we mean something to each other."

"If we do, it is something that has to stop immediately!" Harry snapped. "As I have said, you have your life, and I have no place in it."

"But you have! And nothing you can say can alter that."

There was something very soft in her voice now, and as Harry looked at her and their eyes met, it seemed as though words were superfluous and their hearts were saying things that could never be expressed by their lips.

Then suddenly, he was not certain whether Lucy-May moved first or he did, she was close in his arms and he was kissing her wildly, passionately, so that the barn seemed to swing round them and there was nothing in the whole world but the closeness of each to the other.

Suddenly Harry pushed her to one side.

"Damn you!" he exclaimed. "You are making things impossible, as you well know."

"Why?" Lucy-May asked.

She looked exceedingly pretty, her eyes shining with excitement, the colour in her cheeks, her lips crimson from the roughness of his kisses.

He didn't answer but walked to the door of the barn to look out.

"It has nearly stopped raining," he said, "and I am taking you home. Understand this once and for all: I'm not coming out with you again, so don't ask for me."

Lucy-May ran across the barn towards him.

"I'll not listen to you! I can't lose you...I can't!"

"You have to," he said, "and if you persist in being tiresome I shall have to leave, which is something I've no wish to do."

"You mean...leave your job because of me?"

"I mean I shall leave Kings Wayte, and if you are not careful I shall tell your father why."

"Now you're threatening me," Lucy-May said. "I love you, Harry, and you love me! What are we arguing about?"

"You're too young to know what love is," Harry said sharply. "Besides, as you are well aware, your father has plans that will not be circumvented, whatever you may say in the matter."

"That's where you are wrong!" Lucy-May said. "Whatever Poppa may or may not say, I have no intention of marrying a man I have no wish to marry."

"At the same time, you wish to be a Duchess."

"For God's sake, don't keep on saying that!"

"Put on my coat! Rain or no rain, we are going back to the house."

"You're ordering me about and I don't like it!" Lucy-May protested. "Besides, I want to talk to you ... about us."

"There is no question of 'us,'" Harry said. "You're the daughter of a millionaire who has paid a very considerable sum to rent this house, the Estate, and the services of those who administer it. It is neither right nor proper that you should concern yourself with me in a manner which is extremely reprehensible of us both."

"There's nothing reprehensible about my feelings for you," Lucy-May replied. "I think I loved you from the first moment I saw you by the lake when you were so shocked by my bathing-dress."

"You're not to say such things!"

"But it's true," Lucy-May insisted. "You can't help love ... it just happens. I thought you looked attractive riding under the trees, and when you came near I knew I was right and you were very attractive ... so attractive I've been able to think of no-one else since."

"That's not true."

"It is true!"

"If it is, there is nothing we can do about it."

"Why not?" Lucy-May asked. "However stiff-necked and pompous you are being, you know you love me."

Harry made a sound that was curiously like a groan.

He looked through the open door to where in the far distance he could just see the roofs of Kings Wayte.

"Whatever we may feel," he said after a long pause, "we have to forget it."

"Why?"

"Because I've no intention of deceiving your father, and you know as well as I do that to do so would only make us more unhappy than we are already."

"Are you unhappy?" Lucy-May asked quickly.

"I'm not going to answer that question."

"Then I'll answer it for you. You love me, Harry, as I love you! We belong to each other and nothing Poppa or any other person can say can alter that."

"We have to forget all this nonsense," Harry said. "As I have told you, if you persist in being difficult, I shall have to leave Kings Wayte."

"If you go away I shall follow you."

"Be sensible!" he pleaded. "Try to understand that to go on as we are will make life completely intolerable."

"It might make it that for you," Lucy-May flashed, "but for me it would be wonderful! I want to see you, I want to be with you, I want you to kiss me again."

She moved a little nearer to him.

As she spoke, Harry took a step sideways, saying as he did so:

"Will you behave yourself? I'm trying to act like a gentleman, Lucy-May, but you are making it damned hard!"

Lucy-May gave a little cry of delight.

"At last you have called me by my name!" she said. "I wondered what it would sound like on your lips. Oh, Harry, I love your English accent!"

"I don't have an accent . . ." Harry began.

Then he laughed as if he could not help it.

"Please be sensible," he pleaded. "We are getting deeper and deeper into a morass which will prove disastrous unless we stop."

"All I want is to be with you."

"Which is what you can't be," Harry said. "Oh, my dear, you have to believe me when I tell you we are both playing with fire, and that is something I can't permit you, at any rate, to do."

"Why not . . . if I want to?"

"Because I'm older than you, because I can see the danger, because, if you like, I'm too fond of you to want you to suffer."

"What you are really saying is that you love me."

"I have not said it."

"But that is what you feel."

Harry gave a sigh.

"You're making things very difficult."

"I want to make them difficult, if I can have my own way."

"That is something I don't intend you to have, and incidentally I dislike bossy, authoritative women."

"Then I'll be soft, clinging, and feminine, if only you'll love me."

Harry laughed again somewhat reluctantly. Then he said:

"I don't know what to do with you. I have never met anyone like you, and I suppose I'm bewildered and bewitched. That's why I have to be strong enough for both of us."

"Strong about what?"

"About our future behaviour. It is extremely regrettable that things have gone as far as they have. We will be more circumspect in the future."

"Are you saying again in rather grand words that you won't see me again?"

"Exactly!"

"Then I refuse to have you dictate to me. I shall be bossy, authoritative, overbearing, if you like, but I'm going to see you, Harry, because I can't bear not to."

To her surprise, Harry put his hands on her shoulders, holding her firmly as he said:

"Now listen to me! I was born a gentleman and

I have every intention of trying to behave like one. Whatever you may say, however much you may tempt me, I refuse to be alone with you again. I swear that if you persist in doing what you have done this morning, then I shall leave Kings Wayte and I shall arrange for another man to take my place."

There was something in the forceful way he spoke which made Lucy-May realise that he was in earnest, and she gave a cry of despair.

"Oh, Harry, no!" she said. "I can't bear it! I can't lose you!"

She held out her arms and before he could prevent her she had put them round his neck and was pressing herself against him.

"I love you, Harry! I love you! Now I know that you mean more to me than I ever dreamt you could."

She lifted her face to his, trying to pull his head down to hers as she did so, but Harry resisted her.

He unclasped her hands from behind his neck.

"It's no use, Lucy-May," he said, and now his voice was sad. "In other circumstances perhaps we might have found a wonderful happiness together, but because you are you and I am I, it is impossible."

He looked at her for a long moment, then he lifted her hand and touched it with his lips.

"This is good-bye, my sweet," he said, "and you must accept the inevitable."

"I can't ... I won't!" Lucy-May began.

But Harry had turned away from her and walked to the end of the barn to bring back the horses.

As he passed his coat lying on the ground, he picked it up and slipped it on.

Lucy-May stood where she was, watching him with an inexpressible pain in her large eyes.

When he came back, leading both the horses, Harry made no effort to help her into the saddle.

He knew she was quite capable of mounting by herself, and when she had done so, he swung himself into his own saddle and they rode off without speaking.

The rain had stopped and a pale sun was coming through the clouds. Lucy-May felt there was really nothing more she could say and nothing she could do.

It took them a very short time to reach the front of the house and Kings Wayte looked more imposing and more beautiful, Harry thought, than he had ever seen it.

Yet in a way it was like a dream from another world; a world of unreality, a world which most people thought had now been lost, destroyed by the war.

'Because you are mine,' he thought to himself, 'I have to go on fighting for you, whatever the cost.'

It flashed through his mind that if he married Lucy-May, her money would save Kings Wayte and he would know a happiness he had never expected to find.

Then he told himself that such a fantasy could never be realised.

Lucy-May belonged to a new, hard, commercial world which demanded value for money, and what her father expected for his millions was the Ducal title which he had already arranged.

Lucy-May wanted it too. Yet, like all women, she wished to have her cake and eat it too, which was something he had no intention of allowing.

Everything that was fine in Harry shrank from the idea of making love in a secretive manner to a woman who belonged to somebody else and who undoubtedly thought him inferior not only because she was to marry a Duke but also because he was poor enough to be nothing but a servant in the employment of her father.

"I hope I have enough pride left to prevent myself from sinking to that level," Harry told himself savagely.

At the same time, he realised that pride was cold comfort.

* * *

As Harry and the horses clattered away towards the stables, Lucy-May walked slowly up the steps and into the Hall.

Absent-mindedly she handed her riding-whip to one of the footmen, then without speaking went up the stairs.

As she did so, she felt that her whole world had somehow fallen about her ears and she had no idea what she could do about it.

It was a long time since Lucy-May had felt unsure of herself, lost, and afraid of her own feelings, but that was how Harry had left her.

He had said he was bewildered and bewitched, but she was bewildered too, in a very different way.

She knew, now that she had fallen in love, that she had not realised it would be so painful or that it would present a million problems to which she could not find an answer.

"I want Harry, I want him!" she told herself as she walked towards her own bedroom.

Then she thought of the Duke and her father's determination that she should be a Duchess.

All her life Lucy-May had been adored by her father, and there was a closeness between them which, after her mother's death, had intensified to the point where they were almost inseparable.

It had not really surprised Lucy-May when her father told her he had chosen a husband for her.

It had somehow seemed inevitable, and the fact that the Duke was both good-looking and charming made it seem just like one of the stories that her father used to tell her when she was a little girl and he came to her bedroom to kiss her good-night.

She was the Princess, and the Prince had come to her from a far-off country and offered her his hand and heart, and of course they would live happily ever afterwards.

Lucy-May had been feted and made a great fuss of in America from the moment she had emerged on the social scene.

She had been very much younger than the age at which any English girl would have been permitted to appear, but Mr. Wardolf wanted to have her with him.

Before she was sixteen Lucy-May had accompanied him to many huge social functions, besides travelling in his special train across the prairies and being received with him in many strange and rough places in the western part of the country.

When she grew older there were men who pursued her not only because she was a great heiress but also because she was very pretty.

It had never meant anything to her, except that she liked men because she was used to being with her father and found them easier to talk to than women, the majority of whom disapproved of her.

Then when she had first seen Harry she knew something strange had happened to her heart that had never happened before, and after the first day when they had gone riding she found herself counting the hours until she could see him again.

"I love him!" she told her reflection in the mirror. "I love him!"

She was sure, as she spoke, that there was no argument about that, but what could she do about it?

She imagined her father's anger when she confessed that she had no wish to marry the Duke because she had fallen in love with a man who was very different from the son-in-law he had been envisaging.

Although her father was prepared to give her the moon and stars should she want them, she knew he expected to have his own way in everything else that concerned her, and most especially her marriage.

"These young American men are too brash and too uncivilised for you, my poppet," he had said often enough. "They're civilised on the surface but still uncultured underneath. Frenchmen are too insincere and Italians are over-passionate."

He paused.

"I want to see you married to an Englishman. They make the best husbands in the world, and although we chucked them out of our country, the English still have a great deal to offer us and it would be stupid not to appreciate that fact."

Lucy-May knew he was talking about culture and she realised that her father was unique among his contemporaries in that he had a great appreciation of the arts that were centred in Europe and were very little understood by the average American.

She was not surprised that when he reached London he had spent all his spare time at the National Gallery and the British Museum.

"What do you find so interesting there, Poppa?" she had asked, and he had replied:

"It's places like that which make the English what they are. The Galleries teach me a great deal about art, also about the race who have collected and treasured them."

It was an aspect of her father which she had not considered before, and she respected and admired him for being so frank and for admitting, influential though he was, that there was a great deal more for him to learn.

She knew how thrilled and in a way triumphant he had been when Tybalt Hampton, who had worked for him for a year and whom he liked and trusted, suddenly overnight became a Duke.

At first she had found it hard to accept when her father had said with a glint in his eyes:

"Hampton is a man I trust and would like to have had as a son. Now I can envisage him in a position very near to it, as my son-in-law!"

"But ... Poppa!" Lucy-May had cried in astonishment.

"We are fortunate," her father said, "but then I've always had my lucky streak. Hampton is now a Duke and I want to see you, my poppet, as a Duchess by his side."

The new Duke had left New York in a hurry to attend his uncle's funeral, and Lucy-May had learnt that his inheritance had been as great a surprise to him as it had been to them.

The previous Duke, Tybalt's uncle, had had two sons, of whom one had been killed in the very last days of the war; the other had been wounded but not fatally.

He became engaged to a very charming girl he had known all his life and it was thought that the continuity of the family was safe.

Then quite unexpectedly, it appeared, a very heavy cold had turned to pneumonia and because he had already been weakened by his wounds the young man died.

Tybalt Hampton had received a cable telling him to return to England immediately to take up his position as head of the family.

Lucy-May had known, when he was explaining to her father what had happened, that he could hardly believe the whole thing was the truth and not a dream.

He had actually been so incoherent in his explanations that Mr. Wardolf had asked:

"Are you telling me, Hampton, that now that your uncle is dead you have come into his title?"

"Yes, Sir. I am now the fifth Duke of Stadhampton."

"I can hardly credit it!"

"Nor can I, Sir, but the cable is quite explicit. My uncle died yesterday, and although I was not aware of it, his son, my cousin, died last week."

"A double tragedy," Mr. Wardolf murmured.

"It is indeed, Sir."

"But not to you, Hampton. I imagine you are now a rich man."

"That's very unlikely, Sir. The war has depleted most big Estates and there are also death-duties to be paid, which on my uncle's Estate will be quite considerable."

"But you will be a Duke!" Mr. Wardolf murmured.

It was in that moment that Lucy-May knew he had decided not only Tybalt Hampton's future but her own.

"Do I really want to be a Duchess?" she asked herself now.

It had seemed a very exciting and rather lovely thing to be when she had first thought about it.

The leading social hostesses in New York were all incredibly snobbish.

Any visiting aristocrat from England or France was always feted, quarrelled over by those who wished to entertain them, and inevitably, if they were bachelors, had every important débutante of the Season paraded before them as if they were cattle in a show.

Lucy-May realised that as her father always wanted to win every race, every business venture, every gamble in which he took part, he would also wish his daughter to obtain for him a son-in-law who in rank would outvie everyone else.

It seemed as if the Duke of Stadhampton had fallen into his lap like a golden apple from a mythological tree.

"One of the most important Dukes in England— that's who Stadhampton is!" Mr. Wardolf had said over and over again. "Every door of any importance in the world will be open to you."

"Any door is open to me now as your daughter," Lucy-May replied.

Her father had smiled at her affectionately.

"Only in America, my dear. I cut no ice on the Continent of Europe. I am well aware of that, unless of course I am prepared to pay for it, which is a very different thing."

Lucy-May was astute enough to understand exactly what he meant. She herself thought it would be very nice to make her father so happy, and Tybalt Hampton was an extremely handsome man.

She would also, she was sure, be clever enough not to make too many mistakes when she was a Duchess.

What she had not anticipated was that she would fall in love—and with one of her father's employees!

Chapter Five

"Now that Tybalt is better," Mr. Wardolf said, "we can give the much-talked-about Ball."

"Yes, of course," Lucy-May replied.

She didn't sound very enthusiastic and her father looked at her in surprise before he went on:

"I'll arrange the Band, and you must remind Dunstan to send out the invitations. I believe they were all ready a week ago."

The Duke said nothing.

He thought that Lucy-May's friends did enough dancing without having a large Ball.

They seemed to think of little except Fox-Trotting and One-Stepping, and he had already come to the conclusion since coming downstairs after his accident that it was difficult to distinguish one from another.

They all looked so much alike: the girls all had bobbed or shingled hair and short dresses with low waist-lines, and the young men had a kind of artificial gaiety about them which he knew expressed not only their joy at being alive after the horrors of war but also an effort to escape from the problems which faced them in civilian life.

They certainly seemed carefree enough, but he was perceptive enough to know that underneath their superficial veneer, to most of them the future was a frightening problem which they had no idea how to solve.

None of that worried Lucy-May, he thought, with her huge fortune, her adoring father, and the knowledge that she had only to lift her little finger to have everything she wanted in the world placed at her feet.

It struck him as rather surprising that he had seen very little of her since he had come downstairs. He had felt rather groggy about the knees, and apprehensive in case overdoing it in any way should start one of the blinding headaches which the Doctor had told him he was likely to suffer from for some time.

"You were lucky, Your Grace, to get off as lightly as you did," he had said. "I had a patient last week who had the same sort of collision, and he had a broken nose, required nine stitches in his forehead, and lost two of his front teeth."

The Duke had smiled.

"I am very grateful that didn't happen to me."

"Another time I'd choose your driver more carefully," the Doctor went on. "The trouble with the young men today is that they are all obsessed with speed."

"That's true," the Duke agreed. "And I'm thinking that aeroplanes at least will have plenty of room to fly in without colliding with each other."

"I shouldn't be too sure of that," the Doctor answered, "if all the young fools take to the air!"

They both laughed. The Duke knew a number of men who in the war had found aeroplanes fascinating and undoubtedly would soon be trying to fly the Atlantic or reach Australia.

Lucy-May's guests, however, seemed to wish to do nothing more adventurous than twirl their partners over the parquet flooring to the new tunes which seemed to the Duke to be very appropriate as far as the English were concerned.

Those who had left the Dining-Room where he was talking to Mr. Wardolf had already put the Gramophone on and he could hear the words quite clearly:

Not much money. Oh, but honey,
Ain't we got fun . . .

He looked across the silver-laden table at Lucy-May and was just about to make some joking remark when he saw an expression on her face which surprised him.

She definitely looked unhappy, and he wondered what in the world she had to be unhappy about and if it had anything to do with him.

But before he could say anything she rose from the table and walked out of the room.

Mr. Wardolf looked after his daughter with an air of perplexity and the Duke thought uncomfortably that he was going to question him. However, the servants, fortunately, were still in attendance and after a moment the American got to his feet and the Duke followed suit.

Mr. Wardolf put his hand on his guest's shoulder as they moved towards the door, saying:

"Now don't you do too much, my boy. It takes time to get over an accident of that sort, and if you take my advice you'll rest while you have the chance. I'm going riding."

"I'll be happy to join you tomorrow," the Duke said, "but today I'll listen to your advice and take it easy."

"That's sensible!" the American agreed. "If it's not too far for you, I'd like you to visit the stables and tell me what you think of the horses I've bought. I consider myself a good judge, and I find them exceptional."

"I would certainly like to look at them," the Duke replied.

Thinking that there was no time like the present, he walked across the Hall and as his host went upstairs to change into his riding-clothes the Duke made his way towards the stables.

He didn't walk at all quickly, but nevertheless he found it quite an effort to reach the very fine stable-buildings which had been added, he realised at a glance, by Inigo Jones, in the early part of the seventeenth century.

They were in fact so exceptional that he stood for some time admiring them, appreciating the architecture and the way the red brick had mellowed over the centuries into a warm pink.

As he walked on he found himself thinking that at least this sort of beauty was something American money couldn't transport across the Atlantic.

An old groom appeared and saluted him respectfully.

"I think you must be Hitchen," the Duke said, holding out his hand. "I hear you've some fine horses to show me."

"We 'ave indeed, Sor," the man replied, "best we've ever 'ad in these stables, an' Oi feels real proud o' them."

After inspecting the first two horses the Duke knew they were animals any sportsman would be proud to possess, and he told himself he must compliment Mr. Wardolf not only on his stable but on the excellent advice he had been given in acquiring such superlative horse-flesh.

He moved from stall to stall, finding himself running out of adjectives and merely thinking that he would like to own such animals, but knowing, for the moment at any rate, that he could not afford to do so.

Remembering the horses in his uncle's stables, he knew they compared in no way with these.

Then the thought came to his mind that in the future he would be able to buy what horses he liked and price would be no object.

For some strange reason the idea brought a frown to his forehead, and abruptly he said to the groom:

"Is there anyone at Kings Wayte with the name of Aleta?"

He was watching the old man as he spoke, and he saw that he was about to reply spontaneously to the question, then quite obviously checked himself.

There was silence for a moment and the Duke knew that Hitchen was choosing his words as he said:

"Oi don' think so, Sor," and quickly, too quickly for it to be natural, started to talk again about the horses.

This only added to the Duke's conviction that there was a very definite mystery about the woman who had nursed him the first night when he had been concussed.

He had heard her voice distinctly and realised that he had heard it before, but it was not until Lucy-May mentioned the word "nightingales" that he knew it was the same voice he had last heard two years ago, in the little Temple in the garden of Berkeley Square.

The conversation he had had with the girl he had never seen, but whom he had kissed as a nightingale sang in the trees, had changed his life.

He had gone to the Ball that night feeling near to despair, having spent over two months vainly trying to find employment of some sort.

But any sort of job at which he would have been proficient had either already been filled or, owing to the war, no longer existed.

Tybalt had never got on with his uncle, the Duke, who had done very little for his younger brother except provide him and his family with a small house on the Stadhampton Estate.

Even when he was very young Tybalt had realised that his father and mother had to scrape and pinch and were always trying to make ends meet, while his uncle, as head of the family, lived in considerable affluence.

It was typical that his father never complained.

In fact, he took it as his brother's right that he should have inherited everything while the younger members of the family were, in comparison, to all intents and purposes, poverty-stricken.

The Duke's sister had fortunately married a man

who was comparatively affluent, but his brother— Tybalt's father—had married for love.

Unfortunately, happiness didn't pay the butcher's bills.

When Tybalt had left the Army he had been determined not to go "cap-in-hand" to his uncle, knowing that if he did so he would in all likelihood be refused any help, while if it was forthcoming he would have to be abjectly grateful to the point where it was humiliating.

Pride, however, didn't make it easier for him to find a job, and he had gone to the Ball in Berkeley Square knowing that at least he would not have to pay for his dinner and with any luck he would not be very hungry the next day.

He also hoped, almost against hope, that there might be somebody there whom he had known in the past and who might prove useful with some suggestion as to where he could look next.

This had proved over-optimistic, for the Ball was filled with young people, and although he knew some of the women who were only too willing to dance with him, they had no wish—and who would blame them—to listen to a hard-luck story.

One idea, however, had presented itself to him when he was having a drink with a man with whom he had been at School.

"What are you going to do with yourself, Tybalt?" he asked.

Tybalt shrugged his shoulders and replied:

"I might ask you the same question."

"Well, I'm thinking of emigrating," his friend replied, "not to Australia but to America."

"To America?"

"Why not? They hold the money-bags, and there are all sorts of new developments in that country which they can afford to put into operation."

"I hadn't thought of that," Tybalt said quietly.

"Our industries have been almost at a standstill except for producing munitions," his friend continued, "but the Americans have been going ahead with new inventions, new industrial machinery, and of course new experiments. Something like that should be up your street, as you were in the Royal Engineers."

Tybalt had been about to ask further questions, when his friend said:

"I must go. I'm dancing this one with a jolly pretty girl, and I'm not going to introduce you, so don't ask me!"

"Actually I never thought of it," Tybalt replied, but his friend had already gone.

He put down his half-empty glass of champagne and walked from the house across the road and into the garden in the centre of the Square.

It suddenly struck him that this was the sort of idea he had been waiting for.

It was as if he had suddenly seen a sign-post pointing in a different direction from the way he had been exploring, giving him a definite lead which he had not had before.

And yet insistently a great many questions came to his mind as to whether it would not be a fool-hardy thing to do.

It would take all the money he possessed to pay his fare to America and to live until he found some way of earning more.

There was always the chance that it would prove a useless journey and he would find that the Americans had plenty of unemployed of their own, especially with their own returning Servicemen, without accommodating their allies.

Perhaps he would do better to stay at home and go on looking—hoping that one of his friends would give him a helping hand or that his own ability would find him the sort of work with which he was familiar.

It was then that he had reached the little Temple in the garden and leant against one of the pillars.

He remembered now how talking to Aleta and hearing her soft, rather frightened little voice had in some strange way made up his mind for him.

The Duke didn't really know why. It was not exactly what she had said but what he had felt while he was talking to her.

Then when he kissed her good-night there had been an enchantment he could never forget.

Somehow it was different from any of the kisses he had given or received in the past.

There had been something very special and unusual about it; something that was sheer beauty, a moment of poetry or music that had made him feel that the kiss had aroused a spiritual side of himself which he hadn't even known existed.

When he had walked away into the night, thinking unbelievably that a nightingale was singing in the trees, he had known that whatever happened in the future, there was still a loveliness in the world which no war and no frightening insecurity could spoil.

The Duke had often thought of Aleta when he was in America and had told himself it was because her voice had been such a contrast to the American voices that often grated on him or had sometimes a metallic sound which made him think of money.

He had often wondered if he had made a mistake in not having asked her name and thus made it possible for him to see her again.

Then he told himself that if he had done so, he would certainly have been disillusioned.

She had been part of the darkness and a magic had transformed everything round them into a fantasy so that she existed out of time.

It would be perhaps, he thought, the one illusion he had left that nothing could ever spoil.

America, perhaps thanks to Aleta, had proved amazingly lucky for him.

Only a week after arriving in New York he had met Mr. Wardolf in the house of a millionaire whose son Tybalt had known in France.

It had not been a very close acquaintance, but walking down Fifth Avenue he had remembered that a Marine who had been entertained one evening in his Regimental Mess, when they were at the base, had told him when they said good-night that they must get together after the war.

On an impulse Tybalt had walked up the steps of the huge, ugly brownstone mansion and asked if his acquaintance was by any chance at home.

He was, he was delighted to see a wartime comrade, and Tybalt was invited to dinner that very evening.

It was a large formal party, and when the ladies had left the Dining-Room, Tybalt found himself sitting next to a good-looking American whose name was Wardolf.

He questioned Tybalt about the war, learnt that he had been in the Royal Engineers, and immediately they found a common interest.

Two days later Tybalt was taken on the payroll of one of the Wardolf enterprises.

It was impossible to believe his good fortune.

At the same time, he found that his previous training and the knowledge he had acquired over the four years of war could be valuable to his employer.

Within a year, with a speed that could only have happened in America, Tybalt had risen higher and higher in the particular branch of the Wardolf Empire in which he was employed.

Too, he found himself continually invited to the Wardolf mansion, which was even more impressive than the house in which they had first met.

He had been well aware during that year that any interest he might have showed in Lucy-May, or she in him, would not only have been frowned upon but would doubtless have ensured that he would find himself outside the imposing front door with its brass knocker quicker than he had come in through it.

Then his uncle had died and his relationship with Mr. Wardolf had changed in the passing of a second.

The Duke was not even certain exactly how he

had found himself in the position of being a prospective son-in-law to the American multi-millionaire.

He was well aware that despite his genial appearance Mr. Wardolf was a determined, self-propelling force which it was difficult to circumvent.

He had seen his methods put into operation in Industry and had admired him both for his tenacity and his almost insatiable ambition.

But he found it difficult to relate such a powerful impetus to himself, and he very much disliked the feeling that he was being manipulated.

However, Mr. Wardolf had swept everything before him with the irresistibility of a hurricane, for he had long before determined that his daughter should marry a British Duke.

When one appeared on his doorstep, it had seemed to him like a gift from the gods, and it had never struck him that he might encounter any opposition either from his daughter or from his chosen son-in-law.

"It's fortunate that I have to return home," the Duke had told himself as he journeyed back to England.

'I have no wish to be married,' he thought, when Mr. Wardolf, who was in constant communication with him, informed him by cable that he and Lucy-May were coming to England.

Yet when he went into his uncle's financial affairs, his opposition to Mr. Wardolf's scheme became less forceful.

He'd had no idea how much difference two years of war could make to the Stadhampton Estates.

His uncle had been taken ill at the beginning of 1915, and because no-one had assumed any authority, the expenditure on the upkeep of the great houses and the Estate had continued as it had done over the previous century, but unfortunately there was no longer a huge income to balance the vast extravagance.

It was obvious to the new Duke that a great many things would have to be sold and this presented fresh problems in that most of the paintings and the furniture were entailed.

There were Trustees to see that each successive Duke did not dispose of his inheritance to the detriment of those who followed after them.

Some of the paintings would obviously have to go to pay the death-duties, and the Duke had endured long meetings and arguments, suggestions and counter-suggestions, before, feeling exhausted and more than a little dispirited by the whole problem, he had accepted Mr. Wardolf's invitation to Kings Wayte.

He had seen Lucy-May in London and he was well aware what was expected of him.

Some obstinacy or pride prevented him from actually saying the words to her which he knew both she and her father were waiting to hear.

"There's no hurry," he told himself.

He said it rather unconvincingly, aware that in fact the sands were running out and that if he didn't marry Lucy-May then a great deal of his property would have to be sold and several houses closed down. Far from him enjoying himself in any expansive fashion as the fourth Duke of Stadhampton, he would have to count every penny just as his father and mother had done.

"I have no wish to be beholden to my wife," he had protested to himself, "but what alternative do I have?"

Now Mr. Wardolf had assuaged his pride by his offer to appoint him his Agent in Europe, and the Duke knew well what this entailed.

It would be possible quite legally and openly to make an enormous income—an income which, without his having to call on any of Lucy-May's money, would enable him to run his own houses and Estates as he wished to.

It was a generous offer, exceptionally generous, and he could not understand why he did not feel more elated about it.

And yet, insistently, almost like a tune that kept

on sounding in his mind, he found himself thinking of Aleta; of her hand soothing him to sleep, her voice coming to him in the darkness as he had heard it first that night in Berkeley Square.

As he walked away from the stables the Duke was certain in his own mind that Aleta was somewhere at Kings Wayte.

But if so, why was she hiding? Why had she come to him that one night when he was injured and why had he not been aware of her presence since?

He was quite sure that she was not amongst the guests.

There was not a girl amongst them who had a voice in the least like hers, and if she was not a guest—and it was ridiculous to think she might be a servant—why had he not encountered her?

He walked back into the house, hearing the Gramophone churning out the same music:

> *Times are hard and getting harder,*
> *Still we have fun . . .*

'That's true enough,' the Duke thought as he walked slowly up the stairs towards his own bedroom.

He reached the top of the staircase, which was of exquisitely carved oak and which he admired more and more every time he looked at it, thinking that in fact it was one of the most beautiful staircases he had ever seen.

'If I'm not careful,' he thought, 'it's the sort of thing that Mr. Wardolf will wish me to export to America for him, and I'm damned if I would deprive a house like this just to please some over-rich plebeian who will not appreciate it.'

Then he told himself severely that that was not the way in which he should be thinking of his new employer.

At the top of the staircase he was just about to turn right, towards the State Rooms where he slept, when glancing to his left he saw that there were several rooms, then a green baize door in the centre of the passage.

The Duke knew that this meant that the less important rooms and the servants' quarters were shut off from the grander part of the house.

On an impulse, led only by an instinct and a curiosity which he knew would never be assuaged until he learnt what he wanted to know, he walked towards the green baize door, opened it, and passed through it.

He found, as he had expected, that the passage beyond it was narrower and badly needed redecorating. There was also a flight of stairs going up to the next floor.

He was looking about him when he saw a maid coming down the stairs.

She was a country girl with rosy apple-cheeks, her cap somewhat askew on her tightly pulled-back hair, and the Duke, looking at her, thought she was very young and this must undoubtedly be her first position.

She had almost reached the bottom of the stairs before she saw him and looked at him nervously, ready to hurry past.

The Duke took a step towards her.

"Will you tell me," he asked, "where I will find Miss Aleta?"

It was a fly cast at a venture, almost as if something outside himself prompted him to ask the question.

"She be upstairs, Sir," the maid answered, "in the Nursery at the top of th' next staircase after this."

Then she was hurrying down the passage, and the Duke, with a little smile on his lips, began to climb the staircase.

❖ ❖ ❖

Aleta, having spent the morning helping Mrs. Abbott with the linen, had gone back to the Nursery, feeling frustrated since it was a lovely afternoon and she longed to go into the garden.

Harry had told her so insistently over and over again that she was not to be seen, and she found it nerve-racking never to leave the house except after dusk.

Yet it was agonising to know that he could ride every morning on the horses he had bought, whose unseen virtues he extolled over and over again when they were together, while she could only watch him from the window.

She felt envious that he could go round the Estate and talk to the farmers and their wives, whom she had known all her life, while it was dangerous for her to leave the house.

"It'll be better when the Wardolfs are settled in," Harry said consolingly. "I doubt if they will stay here in the winter, and then you will be able to ride all you want."

It was something to look forward to. At the same time, Aleta longed to be out in the sunshine, to walk through the woods, to see the improvements the numerous gardeners they now employed were making to the grounds.

She only felt safe when the guests had gone to their bedrooms to dress for dinner. Then she would slip down the back stairs and out through a garden-door.

By skirting the lawns and keeping to the shadow of the yew-hedges, she would find her way to the cascade which ran through the shrubbery behind the house to make a water-garden which had once been very beautiful, until during the war it had become overgrown and neglected.

The gardeners were now clearing away the weeds and creeper and Aleta knew it would soon be as lovely as it had been in the past, with little water-falls splashing onto moss-covered rocks and trailing away in a sparkling stream through banks of alpine flowers.

Finally the water reached a huge stone basin

where she had watched the goldfish swimming amongst the water-lilies when she was a little girl.

"It will soon be as it used to be," she told herself every evening as she saw the new improvements.

But she longed to see the garden in the sunlight, although she knew Harry would be angry with her if she risked being seen by Mr. Wardolf or his guests.

"Why didn't I become a milk-maid?" she had asked him at breakfast. "Then I could have worked on the farm during the day and no-one would have noticed me."

Harry had laughed.

"You don't look in the least like a milk-maid," he replied, "except, of course, one in a story-book."

Aleta had been glad that she had made him laugh.

For the last few days Harry had seemed depressed and rather disagreeable. She wondered what was upsetting him.

She had not asked questions. Harry disliked her doing that.

She had tried to encourage him to tell her what was happening on the Estate but she had known when he replied to her absent-mindedly without much enthusiasm that something was perturbing him and she wondered over and over again what it could be.

She had the feeling that he was not happy and that it had nothing to do with the house or the stables.

He had been worried about how much there had been to do before Mr. Wardolf appeared, but that was different from what he was feeling now, and he had been so glad and excited when he had been told to put in the new bathrooms.

Mr. Wardolf had also insisted they should repair the Orangery and bring in fresh orange-trees from Spain since those that had been there for centuries before the war had died.

"Kings Wayte is going to be exactly as it was in Grandpapa's day," Harry had said with a note of elation in his voice. "Think how wonderful it'll be for us when our tenants have gone and we can have it all to ourselves!"

He had spoken in that manner some time ago, but now every day he seemed to grow quieter and, Aleta thought, more depressed, though she could not imagine what was troubling him.

Because she found it impossible to sit idle, she took a linen pillow-case she was mending for Mrs. Abbott from her work-basket and sat down in an armchair by the window.

But after a few minutes the work slipped to her lap and involuntarily her thoughts were back with the Duke.

Ever since she had nursed him the night of his accident she found herself thinking about him a hundred times a day.

It was not only because he was so good-looking. There was something else she could not explain; something that made it impossible for her to forget him, even though she told herself severely that that was what she should do.

"How can I be so ridiculous as to keep thinking about a man who is to marry Miss Wardolf and whom I shall never see face to face or have a chance to speak to?" Aleta asked herself.

But however much she tried to prevent it, he was there in her thoughts and the tips of her fingers still seemed to feel his skin beneath them as she massaged his forehead and sent him back to sleep.

Almost angrily she picked up her work again.

"I must think about something sensible," she told herself, "Harry . . . the horses . . . the farm . . ."

She pushed her needle determinedly into the white linen, and as she did so, she heard the door of the room open.

"May I come in?" a man's voice asked.

Aleta turned her head, then with a little exclamation she started to her feet.

It was the Duke who stood there! The Duke, looking very different from when she had last seen him lying white and helpless against his pillows.

But there was no mistaking his handsome features, except now she saw that he had dark blue eyes that were looking at her in a strangely searching manner.

"W-why . . . have you . . . come here?" Aleta asked.

Her voice not only sounded surprised, but it had a touch of fear in it because she was so astonished to see him in the Nursery.

"I have come to see you," he answered.

"To . . . see me?" Aleta asked.

Then even as he walked a little farther into the room she knew! Knew by his voice, and knew too why there had been something familiar about him when she had stood by his bedside.

For a moment she thought she must be dreaming.

It could not be true, it could not be possible that the Duke was the man she had thought about so often, the man she had talked to in the Temple in the garden in Berkeley Square and who had kissed her.

Aleta had known that she should have been shocked at herself for allowing a strange man to whom she had not been introduced, whom she had never even seen, to kiss her.

Yet she had never been able to feel anything about that kiss except that it was the most enchanting, wonderful thing that had ever happened in her life.

It had been magic, sheer magic! The magic of the star-strewn night, of the nightingales in the trees, of the music, not so much from the Band playing at the Ball as the music in her heart, music which she had thought afterwards must have played in his heart too.

It was not only his lips that had held her spell-bound, but something within her soul, something that had been not of this world but of another.

An enchantment as mysterious and beautiful as the stars, as perfect as the light of the moon shining through the trees.

And now he was here, standing facing her, and she felt as if there was nothing to say and she could only feel as if once again she stepped into a dream.

To the Duke, Aleta was just as he had expected her to be, the hesitant little voice in the darkness, the girl who he had said was the goddess of the Temple and who might in fact have stepped down from Olympus.

She was small and delicate and completely different from the exuberant young women Fox-Trotting downstairs.

Her grey eyes seemed to fill her small, pointed face, and her hair, the colour of the sky at dawn, was swept back in an unfashionable knot at the base of her neck.

And yet there was a rightness about her, a kind of perfection which went with her voice and the touch of her hand. The Duke thought that only a painter like Botticelli could do her beauty justice and she might in fact not be real but one of the nymphs in his painting of Spring.

"How ... how did you know I was ... here?" Aleta asked.

Her voice had all the musical quality he had remembered in his dreams and when he had been unconscious.

His smile seemed to illuminate his face.

"It has certainly been a puzzle to find you," he replied, "and I am very proud that I have been able to solve it. It has not been easy."

"You were ... not meant to ... find me."

"I realised that, and I would like to know why, but it is not really important. What matters is that you are here."

They stood looking at each other until at last, in a frightened little voice that he remembered, Aleta said:

"But you ... must not ... come here. Please ... go away and ... forget that you ever ... found me."

"Do you think it would be possible for me to do that?" the Duke asked. "I have been looking for you, Aleta, for a very long time.'"

There was a long pause before she asked so faintly that he could barely hear it:

"Wh-why?"

"For a great number of reasons, but mostly because I knew when you nursed me the first night after my accident that it was imperative for me to find you as I have wanted to do ever since I came back to England."

"You have ... been away?"

It was a conventional question, but her eyes, fixed on his, were saying, he thought, very different things, things more intimate and personal, and which he answered with some part of himself which he had never before known existed.

"May I sit down?" he asked. "I want to talk to you and I have a great deal to say."

As if his question made her realise that he was there in the Nursery where he had no right to be, Aleta gave a little cry.

"No!" she said quickly. "No. We cannot talk here. Harry might come back, and he will be very angry with me ... or the servants might see you."

There was no mistaking the fact that she was agitated, and the Duke said quietly:

"We have to talk, you know that. Where can we do so?"

"Not here ... not now."

"Then where—and when?"

Aleta clasped her fingers together as if in an effort to make herself face reality. Then something in the Duke's eyes compelled her to change what she had been about to say.

"It would be ... safest in the ... garden."

"Whereabouts?" he enquired.

Aleta thought quickly.

"If you walk across the lawn," she said, "at the end, through the yew-hedge, you'll find stone steps which will lead you to the top of the cascade."

"You will come there?" he asked.

She hesitated a moment, and he said:

"If you don't, I shall come back here. I am determined to see you and nothing shall stop me."

"I ... will come," Aleta said in a very low voice, "but perhaps it would be ... too much for you. You are supposed to rest."

The Duke smiled and she thought it made him look younger, and even more handsome than he was already.

"Finding you," he said, "has swept away any tiredness I might have felt, and it's a far better tonic than the Doctor could prescribe or Mrs. Abbott could force me to swallow."

Aleta gave a little chuckle and he thought it was the sound a child might make, and just as endearing.

Then she said hastily:

"Mrs. Abbott must not ... find you here. Please ... please ... go now."

"I will go as you ask me to," the Duke said, "but you must promise me you will come to the cascade."

His eyes held hers as he spoke, and she said, barely above a whisper:

"I ... will ... come."

He turned back towards the door and when he reached it he said:

"Your Nursery is just like mine, but I deprived my rocking-horse of his tail when I was six years old!"

He left without waiting for a reply, but he heard her laugh, a laugh that somehow was as musical and as lovely as her voice.

It was only as he descended the stairs and

passed through the green baize door that he began to feel triumphant.

"I have found her!" he told himself as he walked down the marble Hall. "I have found her, and I swear I will not lose her again!"

*   *   *

When the Duke had gone, Aleta put her hands to her face, feeling that her cheeks should be burning while in fact they were quite cold.

How could it have happened? How could she have dreamt for one moment that he would find his way up to the Nursery? And yet he had done so, and as soon as he spoke he had revealed who he was.

"How could I have guessed, how could I have thought for one moment," she asked herself, "when I was standing by his bedside, that he would be the man I was always thinking of? Who was in my thoughts almost every night, and a dozen times a day?"

She had known, as she tried in vain to despise the Duke for marrying for money, that he was somehow different from other men.

"What I'm thinking is nonsense," she told herself, "and I have to remember he is a Duke, and he is to marry Miss Wardolf and her millions of American dollars."

Just for a moment she hesitated.

'If I had any sense,' she thought, 'I would stay here and not join him. What are we to talk about? What are we to say?'

Then she remembered the determination in his voice and the look in his eyes when he had said that if she didn't come he would return to the Nursery. She knew that that was exactly what he would do.

And if Harry found him there, there might be a row, or, worse still, the Duke might tell Mr. Wardolf who they were.

If that happened, Aleta was quite certain it would

be impossible for them to stay on at Kings Wayte and they would have to go and live in some cheap Hotel or lodgings. Harry would eat his heart out worrying about what was happening at home, and there would be no splendid horses for him to ride or improvements to supervise.

'I must beg the Duke to keep our secret,' Aleta thought to herself.

Because the idea that he might reveal the truth frightened her, she hurried down the back stairs and out through the garden door.

From here she could take a winding path through thick shrubs until she could move behind the yew-hedge which effectively hid that part of the garden from even the highest windows in the house.

She was well aware that if any of the gardeners saw her they might tell Mrs. Abbott, and Mrs. Abbott would tell Harry, and he would be annoyed that she was running unnecessary risks when everything was built on their anonymity.

"I must be very, very careful what I say to the Duke," Aleta told herself.

Her thoughts seemed to carry her more quickly so that she could be with him and talk to him again.

She arrived at the cascade before he did, climbing up the rough stone steps until where the water came from a hidden spring there was an ancient stone seat on which generations of Waytes had sat and looked at the house below them and thought how beautiful it was.

The long, low Elizabethan building with its pointed roofs and strangely shaped chimneys seemed almost like a precious jewel, protected on one side by the ancient oak trees of the Park and on the other where she was sitting by a fir wood which rose on the steep incline.

In the heat of the day the flowers seemed to glow with a vivid intensity which was accentuated by the lake, golden in the sunshine, and the glimmer of hundreds of diamond-paned windows.

As Aleta seated herself on the stone seat, she thought, as she had all through her life, that no place could be more lovely or be a closer part of herself.

Then as she looked down and saw the Duke beginning to climb the step below her, she told herself that whatever happened, she must prevent him from being instrumental in sending Harry and her away into what would amount to an exile from everything they loved.

The Duke reached the top step with an agility which belied the fact that he had recently been an invalid, and Aleta saw his eyes light up as he saw her there waiting for him.

"You have come as you promised," he said, and it was obvious that he was not in the least breathless from his climb.

"I ... I have ... come."

He sat down on the seat beside her and she expected him to look at the house below them and exclaim at its loveliness as everyone always did. Instead he just looked at her.

Because his eyes seemed so penetrating and almost as if they were searching for something, she felt the colour come into her cheeks.

"Are you really here?" he asked as if he spoke to himself. "I thought I should never find you again, my little Goddess of the Temple."

Her colour deepened and she remembered not only what he had called her but how he had kissed her.

"I have ... come," she said, "because I want to ... ask you ... to beg you ... if need be ... not to tell anyone ... who I am."

She saw the puzzled expression on his face and realised that she had almost betrayed herself.

She had forgotten that the Duke, finding her living in the house, would not expect her to be Aleta Wayte but Aleta Dunstan as the servants had been instructed to call her.

Hastily, because she had to extricate herself from her own stupidity, she said:

"Mr. Wardolf does not know I am here ... that I am staying at Kings Wayte, but I have ... nowhere else to go."

"I'm sure he wouldn't wish you to leave any more than I would," the Duke said. "But if it worries you, then I promise you that no-one, and I mean no-one, will know of your existence from me."

Aleta gave a little sigh of relief.

"Thank you," she said. "It's ... important. ..."

"I'm not interested in why you are here," the Duke said, "but only that you are. You see, Aleta, that night we met in Berkeley Square completely changed my life, and I have you to thank for that."

"You have ... thought about me?"

He smiled.

"A great deal, and I think perhaps you have thought of me too."

Now there was no mistaking the colour that flowed from her chin up to her eyes, and she turned her head away to look at the cascade.

"You are very lovely!" the Duke said in a low voice. "In fact, you look exactly as I expected you to look, as I imagined you in my mind and in my heart."

Aleta did not speak and after a moment he went on:

"I know without either of us having to put it into words that the enchantment we both found that night in the Temple could never be forgotten, but I was afraid."

"Afraid?"

"That I would never find you again, and if I did, I should be disillusioned and you would not be as I remembered you."

"You ... you never ... saw me."

"I saw you in my heart, where you have been ever since."

The Duke gave a sigh.

"I didn't mean to say this, I didn't come here to say it, but now I have to tell you. I fell in love with you that night in Berkeley Square!"

Chapter Six

There was an almost frightening silence, then
Aleta said in a voice he could barely hear:

"It ... cannot be ... true ... you cannot have ...
said that!"

"I have said it," he answered, "although I had no
intention of doing so, and didn't really know it was
true until I saw you. Then somehow my lips spoke for
me."

"It's ... wrong ... and you mustn't ... say it
again."

"Why not?" the Duke asked.

A thousand reasons flashed through Aleta's mind
but she knew as she thought of them that they were
not important, not even the fact that he was to marry
Lucy-May Wardolf.

He was there, and in some strange manner
which she could not explain, the enchantment she
had felt that night two years ago in Berkeley Square
now enveloped them both.

It was as if the words they spoke were not real
words but a totally inadequate reflection of what they
were saying to each other in their hearts.

And yet even that was not the real explanation.

They had been caught up again in the enchantment they had felt that night under the trees when
the nightingales had sung, the magic moment when
they had not been real people but perhaps she had
really been the goddess the Duke thought her to be

117

and he himself had come down from Olympus or from some other planet.

What did it matter where? All that mattered was that neither of them was part of the difficult, perplexing world in which they had lived until they had met each other.

The Duke, as if it was an effort, turned his face away to look out with unseeing eyes at the beauty of the house beneath them and the lake beyond. Then he said in a very different tone:

"I am in love! I love you, but I am not sure what I should do about it."

"There's nothing you can do," Aleta said quickly.

"Why do you say that?"

"Because it is the truth."

"I suppose that as you are living in the house," the Duke said, "you heard I am supposed to marry my host's daughter."

"Yes, I have heard that."

"I have not proposed to her, and actually I have little wish to do so. In fact, I have been manoeuvred into a position from which it would be difficult to extricate myself simply because there will be many repercussions if I do."

Aleta was perceptive enough to realise that he spoke as if he was thinking it out for himself rather than making an explanation to her.

It flashed through her mind that it was because they were so close that she knew what he was thinking and feeling, just as he in the same way felt about her.

That was obviously true when he turned his head to say:

"What am I to do, Aleta? I have found you and now everything that was moving in one direction has stood still and I feel as if I have stepped out of time."

Aleta drew in her breath.

"I feel . . . that too . . . but the world . . . your world and mine . . . has to . . . go on."

"Is that true?" he asked. "Or are we just being conventional and perhaps afraid of the unknown?"

"I am ... afraid that we might do ... something wrong."

"Is it wrong to recognise you as something unique, something which belongs to me and is a part of my life, which I've found not merely after two years but after centuries of time?"

"I thought that ... the first time we ... met," Aleta said hesitatingly.

"We think alike, we feel alike, we *are* alike," the Duke said. "That is why I can no more lose you than deliberately cut off my arm or my leg."

Aleta clasped her hands together.

"We have to ... think," she said. "We cannot ... talk like this and not remember that whatever we do, it will ... involve other people."

She looked at him as she spoke, and her eyes were held by his blue ones and the words died away on her lips.

She felt as if he looked deep down into her very soul, and she had the strange feeling that she was doing the same with him, and she thought she could see in his eyes her reflection and that he could see himself in hers.

"What is the answer?" he asked after a long moment. "There is no-one else in the world except you."

Aleta drew in her breath.

"We must ... try to be ... sensible."

"Why? Why?" he asked. "When one is carried up onto the highest peaks of the mountains and into the burning heat of the sun, one doesn't question how it happened, one just knows it has!"

His voice was very deep as he added:

"Oh, my dear, you are so beautiful, so exactly as I wanted you to be."

"Please ... don't say such things," Aleta begged. "It's going to make it harder ... much harder ... when we cannot ... see each other any more."

The Duke smiled.

"Do you really think that can happen now? I have already said it would be impossible for me to lose you again, and I mean that."

He put his hand for a moment over his eyes, then he said:

"I know what you are trying to make me do when you talk about being sensible, but how can I be sensible when I have been swept off my feet by emotions I had no idea I was capable of feeling?"

"Perhaps it is because you have been ... ill, and everything is a little ... unbalanced," Aleta said in a very low voice.

"That is what outsiders might say," the Duke replied, "but you and I know it's not true, and if we are honest, Aleta, it is not something that has just happened. It started two years ago when I kissed you."

He saw her quiver and her eyes flicker before his so that her eye-lashes were dark against her pale cheeks.

"Do you think I could forget what I felt then?" he asked. "I'll be honest and tell you that I've tried to do so. I told myself I must put it out of my mind, but I remember everything, and perhaps a dozen times a day I find myself thinking of the softness of your lips and the moment when I think we both touched the wings of ecstasy."

There was a note of wonder in his voice which made Aleta look up at him again.

"I thought I ... felt like that because I was so ... young and inexperienced ... but I didn't expect you to."

"Have many men kissed you since that night?" the Duke asked, and now there was a very human and jealous note in his voice.

"There has been ... no-one," Aleta said, and saw the light come into his eyes.

She looked down at the house and said:

"I think we should go back. It'll soon be tea-time and the other guests may be wondering what has happened to you."

"Let them wonder," the Duke said. "They will not find us here."

"But it's dangerous to be together, and Harry ..."

"Who is Harry?"

Again his voice was jealous, so that she felt she must answer him truthfully.

"He is my brother."

"Are the two of you hiding in the house?" he asked.

Then he exclaimed:

"I know who Harry is! He is the Estate Manager whom Lucy-May is always talking about and with whom she goes riding."

"Yes ... that's right," Aleta agreed.

She felt it was wrong to lie to him and she longed to tell him the truth. She longed to tell him who she was and who Harry was and why she was hiding and why it was important that Mr. Wardolf should not know of her existence.

Then she knew it would be betraying a secret that was not hers alone but Harry's.

"What's worrying you?" the Duke asked. "It is because I am asking you questions about yourself?"

He was too perceptive where she was concerned, she thought, for her to be able to deceive him for long, and because she was afraid and also uncertain about what had happened to them both, she said:

"Please ... understand."

"When will I see you again?"

She did not answer and after a moment he said insistently:

"I have to see you, Aleta, and I intend to do so. If you hide yourself away I shall still find you. I can never lose you again, as you well know."

"B-but ... I cannot ... we must not ..." Aleta stammered.

"There is no such word where we are concerned," the Duke said, "and make no mistake, I am somehow going to find a solution to our problems, or perhaps they are only mine. Give me a little time to think, and then we must talk over the conclusions I come to."

"It will be ... difficult for me at the ... moment."

At the same time, she knew it was useless to protest. She wanted to see him as much as he wanted to see her and it would be impossible for them to stay away from each other.

"I'll meet you here after dinner," the Duke said. "Everyone will be dancing and they will not notice if I'm there or not."

It flashed through Aleta's mind that Lucy-May might miss him, but once again it seemed of little account beside the fact that he wanted to see her and she wanted to see him.

"Perhaps you . . . should not," she said. "The Doctor said you must . . . rest."

"I presume you have been talking to Mrs. Abbott," the Duke replied, "but I know nothing would make me feel tired if there was a chance of seeing you."

"Perhaps it would be . . . wise to leave it until . . . tomorrow."

"Do you think I could sleep tonight knowing you were somewhere in the house, unless I have talked to you again?"

The way he spoke made her feel shy and he saw the colour rise again in her cheeks.

"My perfect little goddess!" he said. "You draw me to you by invisible bonds that are irresistible, an unbreakable part of the magic we find together. I shall be here at nine o'clock and I shall wait until you join me."

It struck Aleta that it might be difficult to get away from Harry and she said quickly:

"Supposing I can't come? You must not wait too long."

"I shall wait all night if necessary."

He saw the light in her eyes and said:

"Don't play with me, Aleta. I don't think I could bear it! Once before when I met you I was at a crossroads in my life and you sent me in the right direction. But now I have reached an even more important point, although when I look at you I know there is really no decision to make and the future is already planned for me."

Aleta didn't answer, but he knew she understood.

"I'll go back first," she said, "and perhaps you should follow in about five minutes ... just in case anyone saw us ... together."

"Give me your hand," the Duke said unexpectedly.

Without thinking she put her hand in his and as she touched him she felt a quiver go through her which was almost like a streak of lightning.

She knew he felt the same, for his fingers tightened on hers and although he didn't move she felt as if he drew nearer to her.

"Can either of us fight this?" he asked in a low voice.

At the note in his voice it was as if little flames were moving through her and she felt her lips part and her breath come a little more quickly as her eyes were held by his.

"I love you!" the Duke said in his deep voice. "I love you and there's no-one else in the whole world but you."

It was impossible for Aleta to speak, then he looked down at her hand, crushed by the strength of his fingers, and lifted it to his lips.

She felt his mouth against her skin and it made her tremble while little flames seemed to run through her, burning their way into her breasts and into her throat until they reached her lips.

"I love you!" the Duke said again. "Nothing else in the world has any substance except that."

He released her hand and Aleta rose to her feet.

She couldn't speak, and she felt as if her voice had been burnt away by the fire within her.

Then, almost without her conscious volition, her feet carried her away from him, down the steps beside the cascade until finally, without looking back, she had disappeared among the green leaves of the shrubs.

The Duke watched her until she was out of sight. Then, as if the intensity of his feelings made him want to blot out his sight so that he could concentrate on his thoughts, he put both his hands over his eyes.

❋   ❋   ❋

Aleta reached the Nursery and went into her bedroom to sit down on her bed and wonder whether in fact she had been dreaming, whether everything that had happened had been part of her imagination.

How could it be possible after two years that the man who had always been in her thoughts should be back in her life to love her as she loved him?

She knew now that what she had felt ever since he had kissed her was love. No other man had ever seemed to make any impact on her, so that their faces were a blur and their words barely penetrated into her mind.

She had thought that what had happened in London was just because she was young and shy.

But when she had returned to Kings Wayte, her father's illness and death and Harry's horror at the dilapidation of the house somehow had a strange feeling of fantasy about them. It was as if they were taking place apart from her personally, and she was just watching it all occur like watching a play on a stage.

What alone was real was what she remembered in her heart and what she had recaptured and recreated every night when she was alone in the darkness of her bed.

That magical, unforgettable kiss in the darkness, the song of the nightingales in the trees, the moonlight shining through the leaves had always been with her, like a talisman that protected her from the trials and tribulations of the daily round, the common task.

That had been reality while everything else was of no particular importance because it was not real.

'I love him!' Aleta thought now. 'I love him not with my mind but with my heart and soul, and even if I never see him again after this moment, I belong to him as I have belonged to him already for two years.'

Then she told herself, as she had tried to tell him, that they must be sensible.

Had they any future together? And if so, how could he possibly extricate himself from his position as the future son-in-law of Mr. Wardolf, engaged to marry Lucy-May for her millions?

Aleta knew now without question that he needed money desperately, as she and Harry had needed Mr. Wardolf's rent to save Kings Wayte.

If she had questioned the Duke's motives in marrying when he was unconscious, she now knew the answers without his having to spell them out to her.

The only thing that surprised her was that she had suspected him of having an unworthy ulterior motive, and most of all that she had not recognised him immediately even though she had never seen him when they had been together in the Temple.

She told herself that while her mind was stupid enough to think of him as a stranger, her heart had told her the truth.

That was why she had thought of him so often, why his face had seemed always before her whatever she was doing, and why when he had come into the Nursery she had known who he was at the first word he had spoken.

"I love him!" Aleta said again.

And just as the Duke had said, everything else seemed completely unimportant.

* * *

Lucy-May had gone from the Dining-Room with an expression on her face which made her look uncannily like her father.

She had been wondering all through the meal how soon she could get away, for she had found that the succession of elaborate courses irritated her to the point where she wanted to scream.

She had awakened that morning after a restless night, having made up her mind that she would see Harry however much he tried to avoid her.

For the last three days since they had sheltered in the barn he had evaded all her efforts to meet him, and Lucy-May was getting desperate.

She had not really believed that he intended it literally when he had told her they would not meet again.

She thought not only that would he weaken but that somehow she would prevent him from carrying out what he intended.

Men said one thing but meant another, Lucy-May had found in the past.

She could not really think that anyone who loved her, as she was sure Harry did, would be strong enough to avoid her for more than twenty-four hours at the very most.

But try as she would, she could not meet him.

She went to the stables very early in the morning on the first day, only to learn that he was not there, but had left earlier, the groom told her, for some far-off part of the Estate to which they could not or would not direct her.

The second day when she had not found him, she sent a footman to say she had to speak to him, only to be told that Mr. Dunstan regretted he could not obey the command as, on receiving it, he was on the point of leaving.

Needless to say, the footman had no idea where he had gone.

At first Lucy-May had merely stamped her foot and been determined that he should not behave in such a manner. Then she began to feel afraid.

Supposing she never saw Harry again? Supposing he walked out of her life as unexpectedly as he had come into it?

It was then that Lucy-May knew she was really in love.

It was no longer a question of wanting Harry because he was an attractive man: in fact, she was consumed by a need for him that was so fundamental, so primitive, that she felt that without him she might just as well die since life had nothing to offer her and she was alone.

It had been impossible for Lucy-May, being brought up as she had been, not to realise that men found her fortune irresistibly attractive even though she was pretty enough for them to want her for herself.

She began to realise that she had found a man who was really uninterested in her fortune and was sacrificing her to some absurd principle which she found hard to understand.

"If that's being an English gentleman," she tried to tell herself, "then I prefer an American who gets what he wants without rules and regulations."

But she knew that was not true. She respected Harry for his feelings and in a way she could understand them.

That was the way he intended to behave, and she knew now that he was stronger than she was, and, woman-like, she adored him for it.

"I have to see him! I have to!" she told herself over and over again.

And yet he was so elusive that after a while she began to be afraid that he had put his threat into operation and had really left Kings Wayte, taking a job elsewhere.

"If he's gone, I'll search the whole country to find him," she told herself, then was appalled at the magnitude of such a task.

She got to the point where she even contemplated asking her father to send for him, and then being there when he obeyed the order . . . but somehow she knew that that would make Harry very angry because he would consider that she had cheated.

"I hate his beastly principles!" she cried.

At the same time, she knew he was right, and to use such a trick would be as unethical as pulling one's horse in a race or bumping and boring, all of which were unsportsmanlike and something the English didn't do.

This morning Lucy-May had a glimmer of hope.

She had received a letter from one of her friends saying that she was arriving on Friday, and it suddenly struck her that with her preoccupation with Harry she had no idea what day of the week it was.

"What's today?" she asked Rose, who was tidying her clothes.

"It be Friday, Miss. Another week gone, as my mother used to say when I was young!"

"Surely Saturday is the end of the week?" Lucy-May had remarked.

"Not to us, Miss," Rose replied. "Friday's wage-day, and when the men gets paid that's what counts in the family."

"Wage-day!" Lucy-May repeated in a strange voice. "Are you saying that the people who work on this Estate are paid on Fridays?"

"Oh, yes, Miss. Not those of us as work in the house, o' course—we gets our wages by the month—but the gardeners, the foresters, and them in the stables, they gets paid on Fridays."

"And who pays them?"

"Mr. Dunstan, Miss."

"Where does he pay them?"

"In the Estate Office, Miss, as it's always been done."

"At what time?"

"I'm not quite certain, Miss. I think some o' them as lives the other side o' the Estate comes in early in the afternoon."

Lucy-May had learnt what she wanted to hear. Harry would be in the Estate Office; that's where she would be able to see him.

It seemed to her as if the hours during the morning passed at the pace of snails.

She found herself looking at the clock on the mantelpiece not once but a dozen times, and when she went riding, knowing that Harry would not accompany her, she kept thinking that the watch she wore on her left wrist had stopped.

It was impossible to eat anything at luncheon, although rather than call attention to herself she helped herself automatically from the silver dishes bearing the Wayte crest and "messed about" with the food on her plate.

It was two o'clock when she went along the passage which twisted and turned through the ancient house and led finally, she knew, to the Estate Office in the East Wing.

She had been there only once before, when she had first come to Kings Wayte and had explored the house, finding its innumerable corridors and varied staircases fascinating because it was so unlike any house she had ever seen before.

Now she was concerned only with reaching the office with its maps, its files, and the huge desk at which she knew Harry would be sitting.

As she turned a corridor into another passage, she saw a number of men standing outside an open door.

She realised that they were filing in one by one and she recognised one of the men whom she had seen working on the farm.

Lucy-May saw a chair against the wall with the Wayte coat-of-arms painted on its back, and she sat down.

She knew she must wait until Harry had finished paying the wages, and she only hoped there was not another exit from the office by which once again he might elude her.

Then she saw the men who had obviously been paid coming back out of the room, passing those who were waiting, and she knew that now at last she had tracked him down, and this time he could not escape.

There was not such a crowd as she had first thought, and she guessed that what Rose had said was right and the men from the far parts of the Estate came after luncheon, while the rest would doubtless be there by about five o'clock.

If she didn't see Harry now there would always be a chance later on, she told herself, but she could not endure to wait any longer.

She had to see him, she had to talk to him, and it was not humanly possible to go on suffering as she had been doing these last few days.

The last man went into the office.

When he came out there was nobody to follow him and Lucy-May knew that this was her opportunity.

She waited until he had disappeared down the passage, then she ran towards the office door.

It had been closed by the last-comer and she opened it and went in.

Harry was making an entry in a large ledger which was open on the desk in front of him.

He finished what he was writing, then looked up as if expecting to see another servant who wished to speak to him.

When he saw who stood just inside the door, he was suddenly very still.

"Harry!"

Lucy-May's voice seemed to be strangled in her throat.

Harry rose to his feet slowly, and as he did so, Lucy-May came nearer.

"Harry . . . I have to see you. Why have you been avoiding me?"

"I thought I had already explained that," he replied. "There's no point in going over it again."

"There's every point!" Lucy-May argued. "We can't go on like this, Harry. We have to talk . . ."

"There's nothing to talk about," he interrupted.

He walked round the desk and stood facing her.

"I'm sorry," he said, "I have an appointment."

"Harry . . . please . . ."

"No!" he said sharply. "No!"

He moved towards the door.

With a little cry Lucy-May ran in front of him to stand with her back against it.

"I won't let you go!" she said. "You have to listen to me. You have to!"

"For God's sake," Harry said in a voice she barely recognised. "Stop behaving like this. If you can't stand it, I can't either."

She saw the pain in his eyes, but she knew that he still intended to leave her.

With the cry of an animal that had been hurt she flung herself against him.

"Harry . . . Harry!" she said. "I love you! Oh, Harry, marry me, because if you don't I shall die!"

Her arms were round his neck, pulling his head down to hers, and for a moment he resisted her.

He was stiff and unyielding and she thought frantically and in desperation that she had lost even the power to attract him.

Then his arms were round her and he was kissing her, wildly, passionately, fiercely, as if every barrier between them had broken and there was nothing he could do about it.

He kissed her until she was giddy with the wonder of it, and she kissed him back until it seemed as if they had ignited a fire which consumed them both.

Then in a voice that seemed to be that of a stranger Lucy-May managed to say:

"You will marry me! Oh, Harry, say you'll marry me!"

She spoke against his lips and thought that once again he would hold her captive with his kisses, but instead, as if that question was like a shower of cold water bringing him back to sanity, he pushed her roughly from him.

"No," he said. "The answer is no! For Christ's sake, leave me alone!"

As he spoke he walked out of the room, slamming the door behind him, and she was left staring at its surface, knowing that she had failed and her whole world had collapsed into ruins.

* * *

Mr. Wardolf walked into the Drawing-Room, which had been set aside for dancing, to find practically all his guests doing the Two-Step.

Like the Duke, he found it hard to distinguish one from another, but he did recognise several rather pretty girls who had been with them for over a week and two young men whom he thought rather more inane than the rest.

But there was no sign of Lucy-May or the Duke.

He thought with satisfaction that they must be together somewhere, but then he heard someone crossing the Hall and looked round to see the Duke coming down the stairs.

"Hello, Tybalt," he said. "Have you seen Lucy-May?"

"No, not since luncheon," the Duke replied. "I've been having a rest. Could I now have a talk with you?"

"I will come to the Library," Mr. Wardolf replied, "after I have found Lucy-May!"

The Duke did not reply but went on towards the Library, and Mr. Wardolf looked towards the two footmen on duty in the Hall.

"Have you seeen my daughter?" he enquired.

"Not for some time, Sir," one of them replied.

"What was she doing then?"

"She was going upstairs, Sir."

The footman hesitated, then added:

"She seemed a bit upset, Sir."

"Upset?" Mr. Wardolf asked quickly.

"Yes, Sir."

Mr. Wardolf hurried up the staircase and along the passage to the State Bedroom that Lucy-May had chosen as she thought it more attractive even than the Queen's Room.

It was called the Elizabethan Room and it was furnished very much as it must have been at the time when the house was built.

But, although the Wardolfs were not aware of it, the curtains and carpet had come from another famous Elizabethan house, the contents of which had recently been sold because its owner had been killed in the war.

It was in fact a very attractive room, with two bow windows and an oak four-poster bed carved with flowers and fruit.

Having knocked, Mr. Wardolf entered the room without waiting for a reply, to find his daughter lying face downwards on the bed.

"Lucy-May . . ." he began.

As she turned to look towards him he added:

"What's happened? What's upset you? Why do you look like that?"

"Go away!" Lucy-May cried, hiding her face again in the pillow. "Leave me alone. There's nothing you—can do—nothing anyone can do—all I want is to—die!"

Mr. Wardolf moved beside the bed and put his hand on his daughter's shoulder.

"Now what's all this about?" he asked. "I can't bear to see you looking like that, my poppet."

It struck him that he had not seen Lucy-May cry since her mother died and he could not imagine what had occurred now to get her into the state she was obviously in.

From the one glimpse he had had of her face, he knew that her eyes were swollen and her cheeks were streaked with tears, and something very serious must have occurred to upset her in such a manner.

He seated himself on the edge of the bed and said:

"Suppose you tell me about it?"

"There's—nothing to—tell."

"There must be!" he protested.

"If there was—anything, I'd be—happy and not —miserable as I am—now."

Lucy-May's voice broke on the words and she was crying again—crying in a manner which upset her father and made him know he would do anything, anything in the world, to prevent his child from suffering.

He bent down and pulled her into his arms.

She didn't resist him but hid her face against his shoulder and he held her close as if she were a baby.

"Now tell me what all this is about," he said gently.

"Oh—Poppa—I'm so—unhappy!"

"If it's a problem, you know I'll solve it for you."

"You can't do that—nobody can!"

"Why not?"

Lucy-May didn't answer, she merely went on crying.

"Now listen, my honey," Mr. Wardolf said, "we've been together long enough for you to know that where I'm concerned nothing is impossible, and I mean that! Whatever has upset you, whatever has made you cry like this, I'll find out what you want, or put right what has gone wrong."

"It's no—use—Poppa—we are not in America now—we're in England—and Englishmen don't—think like us."

"You mean it's a man who has upset you?"

Mr. Wardolf's voice was sharp, and when Lucy-May didn't answer, he asked:

"What man? Is it the Duke?"

"No—it's not the—Duke."

"Another man? Who?"

"It's no use my telling you," Lucy-May sobbed. "It'll only make you—angry, and he won't change his—mind."

With considerable effort Mr. Wardolf restrained himself from bluntly commanding her to tell him what she was talking about.

He had tried those tactics with Lucy-May before and they had never worked.

Instead he held her more closely and kissed her hair before he said:

"Now, sweetheart, you're making me as unhappy as you are yourself. You tell me what's upset you, and whatever it is, I swear I'll not be angry."

"You are—sure—quite sure you'll not be?"

"I give you my word of honour. I'll not be angry

with you or the man, if that's what you're worrying about."

"I'm not worried about him," Lucy-May said. "I've—lost him—and he won't marry, me—even though I've asked him to."

Mr. Wardolf stiffened, then he said:

"You've asked somebody whose name I don't know to marry you?"

"Yes, I—begged him to—marry me—but he said no—and I know why."

"Why?" Mr. Wardolf enquired.

"Because I'm rich and he's not. Because he knows you wouldn't approve! He's—too honourable to see me secretly—and he won't marry me. Oh—Poppa—Poppa—what am I to do? I wish I were dead!"

Mr. Wardolf was bewildered, but he knew that the one person he adored in the whole world was suffering as he had never imagined she could suffer, and that made him ask very quietly:

"Tell me who it is that you love."

"It's—Harry—I know you'll be—angry—but I can't help it—I love him! I love him! And as far as I'm concerned—there's not another—man in the whole world."

For a moment Mr. Wardolf was puzzled.

His mind flickered over the young men who were staying in the house, none of whom he could remember being called Harry.

Then he said slowly, as if the idea was quite inconceivable:

"You can't mean Dunstan?"

"I—knew you'd be angry!" Lucy-May sobbed. "But you promised—you promised you'd not be angry with—him."

"I'm not angry," Mr. Wardolf said untruthfully. "I'm only trying to understand what's happened."

As if Lucy-May knew what he was thinking, she gave a little cry.

"If you think he's been playing with me—you're mistaken! It's I who have been pursuing him. I told

him I love him and I know that he loves me—but he
has sworn he'll never see me again—and he's managed to avoid seeing me for three days—and it's been
agony—just agony!"

"And what happened today?" Mr. Wardolf asked.

"I caught him when he was—paying out the
wages," Lucy-May said a little more coherently than
she had spoken before. "I told him I couldn't live
without him—and I asked him to—marry me."

"And what did he say?"

There was a sudden burst of tears before Lucy-
May replied in a voice her father could barely hear:

"He said: 'For Christ's sake, leave me alone!'"

Now she was sobbing again, sobbing in a heart-
breaking fashion, and it made her father feel she
was only a child again, too young and too vulnerable
to face the hardness and cruelty of life.

Then as she continued to cry he said after a
moment:

"What do you want me to do? How can I help
you?"

"There's—nothing you—can do," Lucy-May replied. "If Harry won't listen to me—he won't listen to
you. Only if you told him I'll never have a cent of
your money and you'll cut me off—disown me—then
perhaps—he might realise how much I care."

There was a cynical expression on Mr. Wardolf's
face as he said:

"I promise you I'll have a talk with this young
man, but you know, dearest, that I wanted you to
marry the Duke."

"I know, Poppa, but I wouldn't marry him if
he was the last man in the world," Lucy-May replied. "I won't marry anyone, anyone except Harry—
and if he won't marry me—I'll just remain unmarried
with you for the—rest of my life."

If she had spoken doubtfully it would have been
easier, Mr. Waldolf thought, to discount it as part
of her mood at the moment, but Lucy-May spoke with
a positiveness and determination that was almost an
echo of his own voice.

His plans had fallen about his ears, but he knew, because he loved Lucy-May as he had never loved another human being, that he was not going to stand by and see her suffer without trying to do something about it.

Very gently he laid her down on the pillows.

"Now wash your face, my honey," he said, "then go into the Sitting-Room until I come back. I'll go and talk to young Dunstan and see what all this is about."

Lucy-May hung on to her father frantically.

"You're not to be—unkind to him—you're not to be—angry. It's not his fault—it's mine! I know he would never have—told me that he—loved me if I hadn't said it—first. I pursued him, Poppa, pursued him because I wanted him—because I love him—and one—can't help love."

There was something pathetic in the way she spoke, and, still holding on to her father, she said in a voice barely above a whisper:

"Momma told me that when you and she first met, you had no money—and were only just getting started—but she never for a moment thought about the—future—whether you were rich or poor—all she knew was that she—loved you and as far as she was concerned you were the—only man in the whole—world."

"Leave everything to me," Mr. Wardolf said.

He kissed his daughter's cheek, then walked towards the door.

"I'll not be longer than I can help," he said.

He walked along the passage and when he got to the top of the stairs he called one of the footmen.

"I want to speak to Mr. Dunstan immediately!" he said. "Have you any idea where he is likely to be?"

To his surprise, the footman looked indecisive.

"I said immediately!" Mr. Wardolf said sharply. "Is he in the house?"

"Oi thinks so, Sir."

"Then go and find him and ask him to come and speak to me in the Library. It's important!"

"Very good, Sir."

Mr. Wardolf went down the stairs, and the footman, as he had expected, didn't follow. Instead, he knew, he went to the green baize door at the end of the passage.

Mr. Wardolf went towards the Library and only as he reached the door did he remember that the Duke would be there, and he immediately retraced his steps into the Hall.

He decided he would wait until Dunstan arrived, then take him into one of the other Sitting-Rooms where he knew they would not be disturbed.

He was wondering what he would say. At the same time, he had promised Lucy-May he would do something, but now he was not certain what it would be.

In fact, as he waited, his anger grew against the man who had upset his daughter and his own plans.

The footman returned, coming down the staircase.

He reached Mr. Wardolf's side.

"Oi'm sorry, Sir, but Mr. Dunstan asked me to say that he can't come as you requested, as he's leaving within the next few minutes."

"Leaving?" Mr. Wardolf asked sharply.

"Yes, Sir."

"Where is he going?"

"I don't know, Sir."

"You mean he's going out into the grounds, or going away?"

"Oi think he's going away, Sir. He was packing when I spoke to him."

Mr. Wardolf's lips tightened.

"Show me where I can find Mr. Dunstan."

The footman hesitated.

"Well?" Mr. Wardolf said. "What are you waiting for?"

"Oi don't think Mr. Dunstan'd like that, Sir."

"I don't care whether he likes it or not," Mr. Wardolf said angrily. "I intend to speak to him. Will you show me the way or must I find it for myself?"

The footman glanced round desperately, as if he thought help would come from some other quarter.

There was no other person in the Hall except another footman, and after a moment he capitulated.

"Oi'll show ye the way, Sir."

"You had better do so if you value your job," Mr. Wardolf said grimly.

They walked up the stairway and went through the green baize door and up the next two flights of stairs.

It said something for the amount of exercise that Mr. Wardolf always took, riding and, when he had the chance, in a Gymnasium, that he was not breathless when they reached the third floor.

As he stepped onto the landing the footman said in a voice that showed he was frightened:

"That be Mr. Dunstan's room, Sir."

He pointed to the door, then scuttled down the staircase.

Mr. Wardolf didn't waste time in thinking that the servant was behaving in a very strange manner, he merely walked up to the door and opened it.

It was quite a pleasant room which obviously had once belonged to a child, for there were pictures of gnomes and fairies on the walls.

The man he knew as Dunstan was packing a leather trunk, while sitting on the bed watching him and, Mr. Wardolf thought, arguing with him, was one of the loveliest young women he had ever seen in his life.

As he entered the room it seemed as if the two young people were suddenly frozen into immobility as they looked at him in wide-eyed astonishment.

Mr. Wardolf spoke first.

"I sent a message asking to see you, Dunstan."

"I received it, Sir, but I regret to say I'm leaving. I have business to attend to in London."

Mr. Wardolf was obviously not troubling to listen, for his eyes were on Aleta.

"Who is this?" he asked. "Your wife?"

He saw the expression in Aleta's large eyes, and Harry said sharply:

"She is my sister!"

"And you are both living here in the house I rent? I had the idea that you were staying somewhere on the Estate."

"We run the house for you," Harry replied, "and one of the conditions, although you may not be aware of it, was that you should retain my services as Manager. As it happens, because I own the house, it was a very satisfactory arrangement from my point of view."

"You *own* the house?" Mr. Wardolf questioned.

"Yes, but it might have been embarrassing for you to have known that, so I changed my name, which is in fact Wayte."

"You mean—you are Sir Harry Wayte?"

"Yes. And this is my sister, Aleta!"

For a moment Mr. Wardolf was nonplussed. Then his business acumen came to the rescue and he said:

"I can understand your motives for this deception, but it's on a different matter altogether that I wish to talk to you."

"There's nothing to be said," Harry replied sharply.

"I think there is," Mr. Wardolf retorted.

He looked towards Aleta.

"I wonder if you'd be kind enough to leave me alone with your brother?"

"Yes . . . of course."

Aleta had seemed almost mesmerised by Mr. Wardolf's sudden appearance, but now she rose swiftly to her feet and moved towards the door on the other side of the room.

Before she reached it, she paused.

"You'll not go without telling me, Harry?"

"No, of course not," her brother replied.

Mr. Wardolf waited until she had disappeared, then he said:

"Now listen, Dun—I mean Wayte. You've made my daughter extremely unhappy."

"I can only express my regret both to you and Miss Wardolf," Harry said in a cold voice.

Mr. Wardolf sat down on the bed which Aleta had just vacated.

"You'll understand that I'm a little bewildered at the turn of events," he said. "Firstly, that my daughter should be almost suicidal."

He saw Harry stiffen, and there was an expression of concern in his eyes, before he went on:

"Secondly, that I should find you are not, as I'd thought, the Manager of this magnificent house, but its owner. Why did you rent it to me?"

"I should have thought that was obvious," Harry replied. "I have no money—none at all, and I either had to watch my home crumble into ruins or try to do something about it. Your offer to rent it for a year at a very generous sum came at exactly the right moment."

"Now I understand a lot of things that have puzzled me before," Mr. Wardolf said. "But let us get back to the problem of Lucy-May."

"You can understand that is something I have no wish to discuss," Harry said. "And I'm doing the only thing possible, by leaving Kings Wayte."

"Where are you going?"

"I've no idea."

"You have some sort of employment in mind?"

"No, but I'll send for my sister later."

"You seem to have thought of yourself and your family, if that is what you can call your sister, but what about my daughter?"

"What about her?" Harry asked in an uncompromising voice. "I imagine, Sir, that she's your problem."

"On the contrary," Mr. Wardolf said. "You have brought her to a state of unhappiness that I've never seen before and that's something I can't allow."

"I've no wish to make her unhappy," Harry said

in a low voice, "it's just something that happened. So I'm now doing what I believe to be the right thing in going away."

"It just might look as if you're running away," Mr. Wardolf said.

"What else can I do?" Harry asked.

For the first time there was something young and rather lost in his voice.

"Perhaps we could discuss it with Lucy-May," Mr. Wardolf suggested.

"There's nothing to discuss."

"She told me she asked you to marry her."

"She doesn't understand."

"What doesn't she understand?"

"That it would be impossible for me, whether as Dunstan or as myself, to contemplate life with anyone like your daughter."

"Is that meant to be an insult?" Mr. Wardolf enquired.

"No, of course not!" Harry said quickly. "I thought I had made it quite plain—the reason why I wish to leave the house is that I have no money at all —none! I've sold a great deal of the contents to meet my father's death-duties, and now, unless I am to let the place fall down, fail to keep up the wages of the old servants who couldn't get another job, and fail to pay the pensioners until they die, I shall have to sell the rest of the contents bit by bit."

"It seems rather a pity," Mr. Wardolf remarked.

"Of course it's a pity," Harry replied savagely, "but that's what war does. It bankrupts not only the conquered but also the conqueror. There's nothing one can do about it except try to survive."

"Have you told Lucy-May who you are?"

"No. What would be the point? She thinks I'm in your employment. But it doesn't really matter who I am, the position is just the same."

"On the contrary, I think there's a great deal of difference between being somebody unknown called Dunstan and being Sir Harry Wayte, who, if I'm not mistaken, is the eleventh Baronet."

"And, I expect, the last," Harry said bitterly. "As I have said before, I shall never be able to afford to have a son to inherit."

There was silence, then Mr. Wardolf said quietly:

"Lucy-May tells me that she wishes to marry you."

He saw by the expression on Harry's face that he was astonished that she should have mentioned it. Then he replied:

"I've already told your daughter that that is an impossible idea."

"Why?"

"Because whoever I am, I have some pride. I wouldn't marry a woman for her money or be beholden to my wife for every penny to spend."

"Very commendable!" Mr. Wardolf remarked. "But it doesn't make Lucy-May any happier."

"I hate to make her unhappy," Harry said, "but one day she'll thank me. Besides, I understood she was to marry the Duke."

"She has just informed me that he is the last person in the world she would marry, and if you don't marry her, she'll remain unmarried until she dies."

"She doesn't know what she's saying."

"She has also asked me," Mr. Wardolf went on, as though Harry hadn't spoken, "to cut her off without a cent!"

The room seemed suddenly very quiet, and Harry looked at Mr. Wardolf as if he felt he hadn't heard him correctly.

"Is that—something you would do?" he asked after a moment.

"I'd do anything," Mr. Wardolf replied, "if it would make my daughter the happy, laughing girl she was before she fell in love with you!"

Chapter Seven

Lucy-May was standing looking out the window in the Queen's Ante-Room.

The gardens were beautiful in the sunshine, but she could see only darkness and despair.

She turned round quickly as the door opened, and her father saw that although she had washed her eyes, her expression was still woe-begone.

Then as she saw who was standing behind him, her face was transformed by a light that seemed to radiate from her whole being.

"Harry!"

She barely breathed the word between her lips.

Mr. Wardolf came into the room and walked towards his daughter, but he realised as he reached her that she was looking at Harry as if he were a being from another planet, and there was no mistaking the adoration in her eyes.

"I've brought Sir Harry Wayte with me," Mr. Wardolf said slowly, "so that we can have a talk."

He saw Lucy-May's astonishment and said with a wry smile:

"This, my dear, is the owner of Kings Wayte, and a rather more important person than we thought him to be."

"It doesn't—matter who he—is," Lucy-May answered in a voice he could barely hear, "as long as he—doesn't leave.

"I don't think he'll do that," Mr. Wardolf said

drily, "and I have a proposition to put to both of you."

His daughter looked at him apprehensively and he said:

"Suppose you both sit down while you listen to me?"

As if they were only too glad to obey his command, Lucy-May and Harry sat on the chairs nearest to them.

They were not close to each other but their eyes said things that only they could understand, and Mr. Wardolf had the impression that it would be difficult for him to hold their attention.

"I had intended," he said in a louder voice, "to make a suggestion to Dunstan, as I thought him to be, which I thought he would find interesting, but which I hope will still commend itself in somewhat different circumstances."

Harry turned his face towards Mr. Wardolf, but Lucy-May continued to look at Harry.

"I was very impressed," Mr. Wardolf went on, "by your choice of the horses you bought for me, by the expertise you have shown in managing them, and of course in the way you ride."

"Thank you, Sir," Harry said quietly.

"I realised the horses which you had bought for my stable here were exactly what I require for my ranches in America, not only to ride but to breed from."

He paused before continuing more slowly:

"I think you would find it a profitable occupation to select the sort of animals I need and also to acquire breeding mares and arrange for them to be sired by the best blood-stock in the country."

He saw a sudden excitement in Harry's expression as he went on:

"I have many friends and acquaintances who would also like to buy horses whose pedigree and performance would be beyond question."

Mr. Wardolf smiled before he continued:

"I was going to offer a very large retaining fee for your services, but I think in the present circum-

stances we might go into partnership. I will finance
the enterprise, and you on your part will buy, train,
and supervise our operations. You can also provide
a perfect headquarters for the whole business at
Kings Wayte."

It seemed, as he finished speaking, that he had
captured not only Harry's full attention but also
Lucy-May's.

She gave a little cry and exclaimed:

"Oh, Poppa! Do you mean that? It's the most
wonderful thing I've ever heard!"

Mr. Wardolf still looked at Harry as he went on:

"I imagine that from what you'll make from this
arrangement, Wayte, you'll be able to keep a wife,
who has only a small dress allowance, in comparative
comfort."

Lucy-May drew in her breath.

Now she was looking again at Harry. There was
an expression of undeniable pleading in her eyes and
her hands were clasped together until the knuckles
showed white.

There was silence for a moment, a silence which
to Lucy-May seemed to last a century of agonising
suspense. Then Harry said as if he found his voice
with difficulty:

"Do you really—mean that, Sir?"

"I am not in the habit of saying things I don't
mean," Mr. Wardolf replied, "and while I want my
daughter's happiness, I don't think it would do her
any harm to learn the value of money and to understand what it means when her husband holds the
purse-strings."

His words released the tension in Lucy-May and
she sprang to her feet.

Then it seemed as if her voice was almost strangled in her throat as she said:

"Oh—Harry—please—Harry ..."

She was pleading with him in a manner which
her father thought any young man would find irresistible, and he was not surprised when Harry

turned to her with a smile which swept away the last vestige of the darkness that had been in his face when Mr. Wardolf had found him packing.

The two young people stood looking at each other for what seemed a long moment. Then Harry asked a little unsteadily:

"Will you—marry me—Lucy-May? I'll do my best to make you happy."

She made a sound that was one of sheer happiness, then ran towards him and hid her face against his shoulder as his arms went round her.

It seemed as if they had both forgotten Mr. Wardolf's very existence, until Harry said in a voice that was curiously hoarse:

"I don't know how to thank you, Sir."

"You can do that later," Mr. Wardolf replied, "but I guess right now you and Lucy-May have a lot to say to each other."

He walked across the room as he spoke, and he knew as he stepped out into the passage and shut the door behind him that the two people he had left behind him had forgotten everything but themselves.

It was impossible not to feel a twinge of jealousy, for Lucy-May had been whole-heartedly his since her mother had died.

Yet he told himself philosophically that doubtless there would be compensations in his grandchildren, who would not only take up a large part of his personal life but also become part of his vast Empire.

As he walked along the corridor and down the staircase he was already planning what further improvements he could make to Kings Wayte.

One thing which was very important was to buy back the paintings and furniture which Harry had admitted to selling and which must be restored to the place where they belonged.

Thinking of how this could be accomplished inevitably brought the Duke to his mind.

Tybalt would know how to approach the Sale-Rooms and find out who were the purchasers of the paintings that had been sold. Unless they had been acquired by some Art Gallery, there should be no difficulty in getting them back, if one was prepared to pay handsomely.

He remembered suddenly that the Duke had to be told that he had lost Lucy-May and her fortune, which undoubtedly would have been of great advantage to him.

'It's his own fault,' Mr. Wardolf thought, as if he wished to find excuses for his daughter's behaviour. 'He should have been a bit quicker off the mark in making her a proper proposal, and, more important, in making sure that she fell in love with him.'

As he walked across the Hall, he was regretting that Lucy-May would not hold the rank of Duchess, which he had envisaged for her.

At the same time, with the facility of a shrewd and clever business-man in cutting his losses without unnecessary regrets, Mr. Wardolf told himself that he had in fact acquired a son-in-law of whom he could be proud and who undoubtedly possessed one of the finest houses he had ever seen in his life.

That still left the Duke to contend with, and as he opened the Library door Mr. Wardolf was hoping that Tybalt Stadhampton, for whom he had a genuine liking, would not feel he had been betrayed.

Just as Lucy-May had been staring out the window when he had entered the Queen's Ante-Room, so the Duke was doing the same.

The Library overlooked the smooth green lawns which swept down to the lake, and the Duke was thinking that Aleta was as lovely as the iris growing golden beside the water and the shafts of sunlight as they percolated through the thick leaves of the oak trees in the Park and looked in the distance like nymphs or immortals from another world.

He heard the Library door open and stiffened as if he braced himself for something unpleasant. Then as Mr. Wardolf came to his side, he said:

"I have something to tell you, Mr. Wardolf, which I'm afraid you will not be pleased to hear."

The Duke hesitated over his choice of words and Mr. Wardolf looked at him in surprise.

He knew that he had just been about to say exactly the same thing, but he repressed the words which were already on his lips and said instead:

"I'm listening, Tybalt."

"It is, quite briefly," the Duke said, "that while I deeply appreciate that you have made it obvious you would welcome me as a son-in-law, I find myself unable to propose marriage to Lucy-May."

He spoke quietly and there was a dignity about him which Mr. Wardolf respected.

There was a little pause before he asked:

"Are you prepared to give me a reason for what appears, although I may be mistaken, to be a change of heart?"

The Duke looked greatly embarrassed.

"I'll be honest," he replied, "and say I had thought that such an arrangement might work out, but now I know it is impossible."

"Why?" Mr. Wardolf asked sharply.

The Duke smiled and there was something boyish about it.

"Quite frankly, I've fallen very much in love with somebody else and wish to make her my wife."

This was something Mr. Wardolf had not expected.

"Isn't it rather sudden?" he enquired.

"It is," the Duke admitted. "And I hope you will forgive me for upsetting you in any way. I can only thank you for what you have done for me in the past, and of course I'm prepared to leave immediately."

"Wait a minute," Mr. Wardolf said. "I want to understand what's happened. Are you telling me that you have fallen in love with someone since you came to stay with me?"

The Duke smiled again.

"It seems strange even to me, but that is what has actually happened."

"Then who . . .?" Mr. Wardolf began.

He thought that ever since the Duke had arrived at Kings Wayte he had never seen him showing the slightest interest in any of the girls staying in the house.

Then suddenly there was a twinkle in his eye as he asked:

"I may be drawing the wrong conclusion, but is the lady in question called Aleta?"

He saw the astonishment in the Duke's expression before he replied:

"I didn't know that you were aware she was staying in the house."

"I've only just become aware of it," Mr. Wardolf admitted, "but having seen her, I can understand your feelings."

"Thank you."

The Duke was wondering as he spoke how Mr. Wardolf could have seen Aleta when only a few hours ago she had pleaded with him to keep her presence in the house a secret.

"I am just wondering," Mr. Wardolf said, "if you are aware who Aleta is."

"I'm revealing a secret," the Duke answered, "but I hope I'm not making trouble for anybody if I tell you she's the sister of your Manager, Harry Dunstan."

Mr. Wardolf laughed and it was a genuine sound of amusement.

"So you too have been deceived," he said. "Well, I'm glad I'm not the only one who has been made a fool of!"

"A fool?" the Duke questioned.

"These two young people have certainly been very astute in concealing their true identities," Mr. Wardolf said, "so let me inform you, Tybalt, that your Aleta is in fact the sister of Sir Harry Wayte, who owns this house!"

He saw the undisguised astonishment on the Duke's face and added:

"And Sir Harry is at this very moment proposing, which you omitted to do, marriage to Lucy-May!"

* * *

The Duke awoke and for a moment thought he was alone. Then he saw his wife standing at the window which overlooked Belgrave Square.

She had pulled back the curtains and the moonlight turned her fair hair to silver and shining on the transparency of her white nightgown gave her an ethereal appearance as if she were part of the moonlight itself.

The Duke, watching her, thought that every time he saw Aleta she was even lovelier than she had been before.

Today when they had been married in the Chapel which was part of his Castle, it had been a ceremony that was not only moving and sacred but somehow part of the ecstasy they always aroused in each other.

It was not possible, he thought now, to believe that the happiness he felt could really exist in this world. Yet somehow, ever since he had first met Aleta, she had seemed to transport him onto a different plane from that of an ordinary, everyday existence.

"I love her!" he told himself. "And I'll spend the rest of my life making her happy."

There was so much for them to do together, and he thought that Mr. Wardolf, despite his shrewd business acumen and the reputation he had in industrial circles of being tough, was also a sentimentalist at heart.

Only a man who understood romance could not only have made his daughter happy but also done the same for a discarded son-in-law.

When the Duke had finally understood the strange twist of fate which had not only allowed him to find Aleta but had also brought an almost unbelievable happiness to her brother and to Lucy-May, Mr. Wardolf had said:

"That reminds me, Tybalt, I have a commission for you which I would like carried out as quickly as possible."

"A commission?" the Duke enquired.

"Yes," Mr. Wardolf replied. "I want everything that has been sold from this house tracked down, brought back, and restored to the place where they have belonged for centuries."

The Duke had looked at him in surprise and Mr. Wardolf had said:

"You haven't forgotten, I hope, that you are my Agent in Europe? I'll allow you a short break in which to get married and have a honeymoon, but after that I want you to get to work before other Agents get ahead of you."

The Duke had been silent for a moment. Then he said:

"Are you telling me that you still wish to continue with our arrangement, even though I am not to marry Lucy-May?"

Mr. Wardolf put his hand on the Duke's shoulder.

"I never let anything interfere with business," he said, "and where you are concerned, your usefulness in this particular field doesn't rest on my idea that you would make me a good son-in-law, but on my belief that you are the best man for the job."

The Duke drew a deep breath.

While he had been prepared to sacrifice a great part of his possessions so that he could marry Aleta, it was an inexpressible relief to know that it would not now be necessary.

If they were careful for a few years, very little would need to be sold off the Estates, and once he got them into running order, they would be much more productive than they were at the moment.

As if he read his thoughts, Mr. Wardolf said briskly:

"Well, that's settled, and there's one good thing about all this—I shall not have to bother to find you a wedding-present. Your Canalettos and the Van Dyke have only to be rehung."

"I don't know how to thank you..." the Duke began, but Mr. Wardolf brushed his words aside.

"We both have a great deal to do," he said,

"and the first is to order a bottle of champagne with which to celebrate."

It all seemed rather like a fairy-story, the Duke thought now, and he remembered that Aleta had said the same thing when he had gone upstairs to the Nursery to tell her what had occurred.

He had walked in to find her sitting as she had been before when he had first found her, in the chair by the window.

He had guessed that she had been expecting to see Harry, and when he came into the room she sprang to her feet with the startled grace of the fawns outside in the Park.

He had stood looking at her and because he could find no better way to express his happiness and the wonder of the future that lay before them, he merely held out his arms.

As if Aleta too sensed instinctively that there was no need for words, she ran towards him.

He held her very close, his lips found hers, and he kissed her as he had done in the darkness of the Temple, and found that the magic and rapture was still there, but even more intense, more wonderful.

The kissed until they both felt as if once again they were swept up into the sky and were no longer mortal but part of an ecstasy that could only be Divine.

Then at last as Aleta hid her face against him and her whole body quivered with the rapture that possessed them both, the Duke said:

"I love you! And now, my darling, I'm free to ask you to marry me—but quickly. It is impossible for me to live without your becoming mine as you have been since the beginning of time."

"I . . . I can . . . marry you?"

He could barely hear the words, but the lilt in Aleta's voice was unmistakable.

"You will be my wife," the Duke said, "and then, darling, everything in my world will be entirely different because we are together."

"It is . . . what I want," Aleta said, "to be . . . with you . . . to love you."

He kissed her again, and it was a very long time before they came back to reality to tell each other everything that had happened since that first night when they had met in Berkeley Square.

It seemed somehow fate that Stadhampton House in London should actually be one of the great houses in that very special Square which meant so much to them.

When the Duke had told Aleta it was obvious that they must spend the first night of their honeymoon there, she had said:

"I can imagine nothing more ... wonderful than to be your wife and ... to be with you ... anywhere in the world ... but to be where we first met ... and know that marvellous, perfect magic as the nightingales sing, would be just like being part of a fairytale."

"That's what we are," the Duke replied. "And no-one, my darling, could look more like a fairy Princess than you."

"I love you!" Aleta said. "And ... everything to do with ... you is ... enchanted."

"That's what I wanted to say to you!" the Duke protested.

Then he found it easier to express his feelings with kisses rather than words.

* * *

Lucy-May wanted to wait to be married for just a few weeks, until her friends and some of her relations could come from New York to be present.

The Duke, having declared that he had no intention of waiting for anyone, had gone from Kings Wayte to his Castle to make arrangements for his wedding.

Two days later, Harry had taken Aleta and the Wardolfs to the Castle and found it magnificent and beautiful, although different in every way from Kings Wayte.

All that was left of the Norman building, which

had been a stronghold of the Barons who had forced the Magna Carta upon a reluctant King, was a grey tower.

Attached to it was a Georgian house designed by Robert Adam.

The Duke explained that the first holder of the Dukedom had commissioned Adam to pull down the buildings that over the centuries had been added to the original Keep, and provide a house that he thought would be a fitting background for his dignity and consequence.

Money had been no object, and Stadhampton Castle was certainly a fine example of the Palladian style with its huge high rooms, painted ceilings, and surmounting dome.

Mr. Wardolf was certainly extremely impressed.

The Castle was in good repair and comfortably equipped, with the exception, of course, that there was a scarcity of bathrooms, while Kings Wayte had so much to be done to it.

Now it would belong to Lucy-May and he knew its full restoration would keep him interested for the whole year of his tenancy.

The Duke, as he was in mourning, was not obliged to invite outsiders to his wedding-ceremony, which was exactly the way he and Aleta wanted it.

When she came into the Chapel on Harry's arm, he thought nothing could be better than that there were no curious eyes to stare at them.

To the Duke, Aleta was the embodiment of everything that was perfect, and when he saw the love in her eyes, he knew that he was the most fortunate man in the world.

Her happiness seemed to light up the whole Chapel, and when he put the ring on her finger he felt that they were both trembling with the rapture of belonging to each other and nothing would ever part them, either now or in eternity.

They had been driven to London in the comfort and safety of a Rolls-Royce which Mr. Wardolf had just bought and which he loaned them for the occasion.

The Duke half-regretted that he couldn't drive Aleta behind his own horses, but journeying by car was quicker and, he thought, more comfortable for her, and that was all that mattered.

He had held her hand and felt as they sped through the countryside, driven by an experienced chauffeur, that they were being carried away into a world where there was only beauty, music, and poetry, and nothing harsh or discordant could encroach on their happiness.

He had known this was true when after a quiet and intimate dinner in Stadhampton House, waited on by old servants who had known his father and mother, he had taken Aleta by the hand and drawn her out through the front door, across the quiet street, and into the garden in the Square.

As if nature had deliberately reconstructed what had happened two years ago, it was a star-strewn night with a young moon creeping up into the sky.

It shone through the thick leaves of the high trees so that they could just see the little path which led through the garden towards the Temple.

Now there were roses and honeysuckle in bloom where there had been lilac and syringa, but otherwise the garden seemed little changed.

The Georgian vase on top of the Temple gleamed in the moonlight, the pillars were very white, and there was the same darkness inside where the Duke had discovered a shy girl who had slipped away from a Ball because she had no partners.

From a house on the other side of the Square there was the sound of music. A faintly familiar tune was wafting on the warm air:

> *. . . there's nothing surer*
> *The rich get rich and the poor get poorer,*
> *In the meantime, in between time,*
> *Ain't we got fun!*

But both Aleta and the Duke knew that the music which they heard was in their hearts.

They walked into the Temple and just for a moment they stood side by side, seeing nothing, not touching each other, but waiting, as if they listened for the fluttering wings of the angels which Aleta had been sure were present at their marriage.

Then slowly, as if he must savour every moment of its wonder, the Duke drew his wife into his arms and his lips came down on hers.

He kissed her until she became one with him and they were indivisible, their minds, their hearts, and their souls entwined until they were complete in one person. . . .

A long time later the Duke raised his head and asked in a voice that was curiously unsteady:

"You love me, my darling?"

"I love you!" Aleta whispered. "And, Tybalt . . . I can hear the . . . nightingales singing as they sang the . . . first time you . . . kissed me."

"They will always sing for us," the Duke said.

Then he was kissing her again until, as if they understood the need, one for the other, they walked back to the house, with his arm round her.

Because she had awakened in him everything that was fine and spiritual and had inspired him since the first moment they had met, the Duke had been half-afraid that his more human desire for Aleta as a woman might shock or frighten her.

But when he held her in his arms in the great carved bed which had been used by the Stadhampton family for many generations, he found that the fire within him had awakened a little fire in her.

He had been very gentle, but their love had been complete. Pure and innocent though Aleta was, she loved him enough to think that anything he did was right and their love made it part of the Divine.

"Do you still love me?" he had asked.

"Oh, Tybalt, you know I do."

"You excite me so wildly, my precious."

"I . . . want to . . . excite you . . . as you excite . . . me."

"That is what I prayed I might do, my beautiful little goddess."

" 'Making love' is so . . . wonderful . . . like flying up to the . . . stars."

"My precious, you are sure that is how you felt?"

"Quite . . . quite . . . sure, and the nightingales were . . . singing and . . . I am certain the angels were . . . too."

The Duke had held Aleta closer still and said a prayer of thankfulness in his heart.

Looking at her now, standing in the moonlight, he told himself that no man in the world had ever been more blessed.

Aleta must have been aware, without his saying anything, that he was awake and that his eyes were on her, for she turned her head and with a smile that illuminated her whole face she exclaimed:

"It's so lovely!"

"And so are you, my darling."

"Come and look."

"I am quite content to look at you."

"I heard the nightingales and I wondered if I could see them. Everything is silver in the moonlight, and it looks like fairy-land."

"You can tell me about it," the Duke said, "but I want you to come back to me. I'm afraid you might slip away into the night and I shall lose you again."

Aleta gave a little laugh.

"You could never do that."

"Come here!" the Duke commanded.

Without waiting to close the curtains, she ran back to him and he pulled her into bed beside him.

He held her close and said:

"Are you real? I was afraid just now that you would turn out to be really the goddess I thought you to be when we first met, and you might disappear into the sky from where you came while I was left looking for you for the rest of my life."

"I am real . . . and yet I am . . . so happy that I'm afraid it is all a . . . dream and I shall wake up to find that you are . . . still the man whom I have never seen but who . . . kissed me in the . . . dark."

"It's not a dream, my precious, as I shall prove to you over and over again," the Duke replied. "And I was thinking how very lucky we were to have found each other again by chance and we must never take such risks again."

"Perhaps it was not by chance," Aleta said in a soft voice. "I think the . . . magic you have for me, and I for you, will always . . . draw us together even if we were a world apart."

"But we are not!" the Duke said quickly. "You are here, my lovely one, and I can touch you, kiss you, and make love to you because you are my wife."

She made a little sound of happiness and said:

"Sometimes I frighten myself by thinking that when we met again you might have been already married to Lucy-May."

"You are not to think about it," the Duke commanded, "and she will be very happy with Harry."

"She'll do everything he wants because she loves him, as I love you! But, darling . . . no-one could love anybody as . . . much as I . . . love you!"

The Duke drew her closer.

"That's what I want you to say to me, not once but over and over again," he said. "But 'love' is such an inadequate word to express what I feel for you. I adore you, I worship you, and you fill my whole world to the exclusion of everything else."

"When I think of how much you were prepared to give up for me," Aleta said, "I feel very . . . very humble. Suppose in time I . . . disappoint you?"

The Duke kissed her hair.

"You'll never do that," he said, "and, darling, I need your help in all the work I have to do for Mr.

Wardolf, the difficulty being that none of the paintings I'm going to buy for him will look half as beautiful as you, and I shall think none of them good enough to hang in his future Art Gallery."

Aleta gave a little laugh before she said:

"I want you to think me beautiful, but when I remember how important you are, I am afraid I shall make a very inadequate... Duchess. How can I shine amongst all the famous and lovely women we will meet at Buckingham Palace and all the social functions which we have to attend?"

"Which we *will* attend, because I want to show the world what a beautiful wife I have," the Duke said firmly. "But as we shall also have a great deal of serious business to attend to, we will not waste too much time on them."

"I'm glad about that," Aleta said. "All I really want is to be with you... for you to teach me about the... things that interest you... and to let me help you."

"At least we shall do a great deal of travelling," the Duke said. "I want to show you Paris, Vienna, and of course Rome."

"Oh, Tybalt, it sounds so wonderful, but promise we can come back here in between the trips to... listen to the... nightingales. Our nightingales that sing of our... love."

"We'll always do that," the Duke promised. "Although Mr. Wardolf has quite a considerable claim on my time, he can't have all of it. I want a home, Aleta, and only you can make that for me."

"The Castle is very... big," Aleta said in a small voice.

Then she added so softly that he could barely hear:

"But... perhaps when we have lots of... children, they'll find it a wonderful place... to play Hide-and-Seek and..."

There was no chance to say any more, for the Duke was kissing her—kissing her so that everything she was about to say slipped away from her mind.

She felt his hand touching her body and felt, as she quivered with a wild excitement, that the moonlight flooding the room was drawing them high up into the starlit sky.

"I love you, my darling," the Duke said in his deep voice. "I love you!"

Then he was kissing her until Aleta felt as if the moonlight was running through her body, changing from silver to flame and burning in the same way that she knew a fire within the Duke was burning.

"I love . . . you! I love . . . you!" she whispered.

But she knew there were no words, and the enchantment, the ecstasy, and the wonder they felt could only be expressed in the song of the nightingales.

ABOUT THE AUTHOR

BARBARA CARTLAND, the world's most famous romantic novelist, who is also an historian, playwright, lecturer, political speaker and television personality, has now written over 200 books.

She has also had many historical works published and has written four autobiographies as well as the biographies of her mother and that of her brother Ronald Cartland, who was the first Member of Parliament to be killed in the last war. This book has a preface by Sir Winston Churchill.

Barbara Cartland has sold 100 million books over the world, more than half of these in the U.S.A. She broke the world record in 1975 by writing twenty books, and her own record in 1976 with twenty-one. In addition, her album of love songs has just been published, sung with the Royal Philharmonic Orchestra.

In private life, Barbara Cartland, who is a Dame of the Order of St. John of Jerusalem, has fought for better conditions and salaries for Midwives and Nurses. As President of the Royal College of Midwives (Hertfordshire Branch), she has been invested with the first Badge of Office ever given in Great Britain, which was subscribed to by the Midwives themselves. She has also championed the cause for old people and founded the first Romany Gypsy Camp in the world.

Barbara Cartland is deeply interested in Vitamin Therapy and is President of the British National Association for Health.

BARBARA CARTLAND
PRESENTS
THE ANCIENT WISDOM SERIES

The world's all-time bestselling author of romantic fiction, Barbara Cartland, has established herself as High Priestess of Love in its purest and most traditionally romantic form.

"We have," she says, "in the last few years thrown out the spiritual aspect of love and concentrated only on the crudest and most debased sexual side.

"Love at its highest has inspired mankind since the beginning of time. Civilization's greatest pictures, music, prose and poetry have all been written under the influence of love. This love is what we all seek despite the temptations of the sensuous, the erotic, the violent and the perversions of pornography.

"I believe that for the young and the idealistic, my novels with their pure heroines and high ideals are a guide to happiness. Only by seeking the Divine Spark which exists in every human being, can we create a future built on the foundation of faith."

Barbara Cartland is also well known for her Library of Love, classic tales of romance, written by famous authors like Elinor Glyn and Ethel M. Dell, which have been personally selected and specially adapted for today's readers by Miss Cartland.

"These novels I have selected and edited for my 'Library of Love' are all stories with which the readers can identify themselves and also be assured that right will triumph in the end. These tales elevate and activate the mind rather than debase it as so many modern stories do."

Now, in August, Bantam presents the first four novels in a new Barbara Cartland Ancient Wisdom series. The books are THE FORBIDDEN CITY by Barbara Cartland, herself; THE ROMANCE OF TWO WORLDS by Marie Corelli; THE HOUSE OF FULFILLMENT by L. Adams Beck; and BLACK LIGHT by Talbot Mundy.

"Now I am introducing something which I think is of vital importance at this moment in history. Following my own autobiographical book I SEEK THE MIRACULOUS, which Dutton is publishing in hardcover this summer, I am offering those who seek 'the world behind the world' novels which contain, besides a fascinating story, the teaching of Ancient Wisdom.

"In the snow-covered vastnesses of the Himalayas, there are lamaseries filled with manuscripts which have been kept secret for century upon century. In the depths of the tropical jungles and the arid wastes of the deserts, there are also those who know the esoteric mysteries which few can understand.

"Yet some of their precious and sacred knowledge has been revealed to writers in the past. These books I have collected, edited and offer them to those who want to look beyond this greedy, grasping, materialistic world to find their own souls.

"I believe that Love, human and divine, is the jail-breaker of that prison of selfhood which confines and confuses us . . .

"I believe that for those who have attained enlightenment, super-normal (not super-human) powers are available to those who seek them."

All Barbara Cartland's own novels and her Library of Love are available in Bantam Books, wherever paperbacks are sold. Look for her Ancient Wisdom Series to be available in August.

Barbara Cartland's Library of Love

The World's Great Stories of Romance Specially Abridged by Barbara Cartland For Today's Readers.

☐ 11465	**GREATHEART** by Ethel M. Dell	$1.50
☐ 11895	**HIS OFFICIAL FIANCEE** by Berta Ruck	$1.50
☐ 12140	**THE LION TAMER** by E. M. Hull	$1.50
☐ 12436	**LEAVE IT TO LOVE** by Pamela Wynne	$1.50
☐ 11816	**THE PRICE OF THINGS** by Elinor Glyn	$1.50
☐ 11821	**TETHERSTONES** by Ethel M. Dell	$1.50
☐ 11815	**ASHES OF DESIRE**	$1.50
☐ 11892	**AMATEUR GENTLEMAN**	$1.50

Buy them at your local bookstore or use this handy coupon for ordering:

Bantam Books, Inc., Dept. BC, 414 East Golf Road, Des Plaines, Ill. 60016

Please send me the books I have checked above. I am enclosing $_____
(please add 75¢ to cover postage and handling). Send check or money order
—no cash or C.O.D.'s please.

Mr/Mrs/Miss_____

Address_____

City_____State/Zip_____

BC—7/79

Please allow four weeks for delivery. This offer expires 1/80.

Barbara Cartland

The world's bestselling author of romantic fiction. Her stories are always captivating tales of intrigue, adventure and love.

☐	12841	THE DUKE AND THE PREACHER'S DAUGHTER	$1.50
☐	12569	THE GHOST WHO FELL IN LOVE	$1.50
☐	12567	THE DRUMS OF LOVE	$1.50
☐	12576	ALONE IN PARIS	$1.50
☐	12638	THE PRINCE AND THE PEKINGESE	$1.50
☐	12637	A SERPENT OF SATAN	$1.50
☐	11101	THE OUTRAGEOUS LADY	$1.50
☐	11169	THE DRAGON AND THE PEARL	$1.50
☐	11962	A RUNAWAY STAR	$1.50
☐	11690	PASSION AND THE FLOWER	$1.50
☐	12292	THE RACE FOR LOVE	$1.50
☐	12566	THE CHIEFTAIN WITHOUT A HEART	$1.50

Barbara Cartland

The world's bestselling author of romantic fiction. Her stories are always captivating tales of intrigue, adventure and love.

☐	11372	LOVE AND THE LOATHSOME LEOPARD	$1.50
☐	11410	THE NAKED BATTLE	$1.50
☐	11512	THE HELL-CAT AND THE KING	$1.50
☐	11537	NO ESCAPE FROM LOVE	$1.50
☐	11580	THE CASTLE MADE FOR LOVE	$1.50
☐	11579	THE SIGN OF LOVE	$1.50
☐	11595	THE SAINT AND THE SINNER	$1.50
☐	11649	A FUGITIVE FROM LOVE	$1.50
☐	11797	THE TWISTS AND TURNS OF LOVE	$1.50
☐	11801	THE PROBLEMS OF LOVE	$1.50
☐	11751	LOVE LEAVES AT MIDNIGHT	$1.50
☐	11882	MAGIC OR MIRAGE	$1.50
☐	10712	LOVE LOCKED IN	$1.50
☐	11959	LORD RAVENSCAR'S REVENGE	$1.50
☐	11488	THE WILD, UNWILLING WIFE	$1.50
☐	11555	LOVE, LORDS, AND LADY-BIRDS	$1.50

Buy them at your local bookstore or use this handy coupon: